DEAD MAN'S SECRET

"Oh, I don't understand," Annabel said. "I'm going to forget about it till Mum gets back. Then I'm going to tell her everything. Come on, let's go."

"Not quite yet," said a soft voice.

They spun round. In the doorway was Brogden, smiling, and in his hand was a shotgun he had found propped in the corner of Uncle Tom's bedroom.

He came into the room and kicked it shut with his heel.

He didn't want to hurt them. He had sisters of his own, and even though he didn't get on with them very well, he wouldn't have liked it if somebody had harmed them. The shotgun wasn't loaded, but the girls weren't to know that; all he wanted was to keep them quiet and still while he searched for what he wanted. "Now you *are* going to be good girls, and do as I say, aren't you?" he said softly.

Also in the Mystery Thriller series:

DEAD MAN'S SECRET

by
LINDA ALLEN
Illustrated by Graham Potts

Hippo Books
Scholastic Publications Limited
London

Scholastic Publications Ltd.,
10 Earlham Street, London WC2H 9RX, UK

Scholastic Inc.,
730 Broadway, New York, NY 10003, USA

Scholastic Tab Publications Ltd.,
123 Newkirk Road, Richmond Hill,
Ontario L4C 3G5, Canada

Ashton Scholastic Pty Ltd.,
P O Box 579, Gosford, New South Wales,
Australia

Ashton Scholastic Ltd.,
165 Marua Road, Panmure, Auckland 6,
New Zealand

First published by Scholastic Publications Ltd., 1991

Text copyright © Linda Allen, 1991
Illustration copyright © Graham Potts, 1991

ISBN 0 590 76282 6

Typeset by AKM Associates (UK) Ltd., Southall, London
Printed by Cox & Wyman Ltd., Reading, Berks

Chapter One

Nobody thought much about it when Annabel's uncle was killed rock-climbing in Wales. Her friends were sorry but, as they said, he must have known the risks involved.

After all, any kind of sport could be dangerous. There was a plaque on the wall at their school to the memory of a boy called Andrew Crawshaw, killed by a wildly-thrown discus one year on sports day. Such things happen if rules are not strictly obeyed. That was sport for you. As to Annabel's uncle, he could just as easily have been killed if he had stayed at home – crossing the road or falling downstairs. All this was said as a sort of consolation to Annabel, but she only nodded and remained silent.

Nick Lestor had been Annabel's mother's brother.

He had lived in a flat in River Street, and was considered a bit of a loner. Annabel's friends had met him once or twice at her house and had got on all right with him. They thought of him as just an ordinary bloke who worked at Fisher's Engineering. It didn't occur to anybody that he was the sort of man who had foreign connections and had been breaking the law without detection ever since he was seventeen years old. Not even Annabel or her mother suspected that.

Annabel had a day off school to attend the funeral. When she came back she didn't talk about it much, but those who knew her best, her special friends, Julie and Simon, thought she had taken it quite badly. They talked about other things to take her mind off it and hoped that she would soon get over the shock.

One day, about a week after the funeral, Annabel and her friends met at the school gates after school. They had done this ever since their days at primary school. The three of them had grown up together in the same close and had never had a serious quarrel. It was often said that they were more like a brother and two sisters than just friends. Although at the time of Nick's death the two girls were both fourteen, they were in different classes at school because of the way their birthdays fell. Simon was in a higher class than both of them, because he was nearly sixteen. He didn't have a lot of time to spare because he had exams coming up, but he enjoyed the walk home with the girls. It was pleasant and relaxing before he got down to his homework.

"Simon, can you spare a few minutes before we go home?" Annabel asked. "Julie and I are going round to Uncle Nick's flat to collect some things, and we'd feel safer if you were with us."

"Safer?" echoed Simon as they set off in the direction of River Street.

"Yes, well," Annabel said, "it's a bit creepy in there now it's all shut up. I went on my own two days ago and I had a feeling I was being watched."

Simon tried to laugh her out of her apprehension. "Go on!" he said. "Don't tell me you believe in ghosts!"

"If I did, I wouldn't be afraid of Uncle Nick's ghost. He never did me any harm. But I don't mean that. I felt as if somebody was watching me from outside."

"Well, there are some creeps about," said Simon, "but don't worry. If we stick together we'll be okay."

"Did you see anybody?" put in Julie.

"No," Annabel admitted, "but there are some lock-up garages over on the other side of the yard and there were one or two people around. I don't think any of them took much notice of me, but I felt as if somebody else was hanging around somewhere where I couldn't see them. Oh, it's stupid, I know, but I just got the shivers. Haven't you ever had that feeling?"

"Yes, I have," Julie said.

"What are you going for, anyway?" asked Simon, to change the subject. "What is it you're going to collect?"

"Just little things that Uncle Nick had in his

3

drawers. Mum's cleared out all his personal things –
his old pay slips, tax records, stuff like that – but she
said if there was anything I wanted before she got the
dealers in I'd better get it soon. Somebody's after the
flat and they'll be wanting to move in. It won't take
long," she finished, with an apologetic look.

'That's okay," Simon said. "I don't mind."

When they reached the flat Annabel unlocked the
door and they went inside. Julie shivered. She
understood what Annabel meant when she said it was
creepy. Julie had a secret fear that there might, just
might, be ghosts around, whatever anybody said.
What if the dead man had some objection to anybody
having his things? She kept very close to the other
two as they walked through the hall into the living
room.

Simon began to look at the records in the cabinet
next to the music centre. He didn't think there would
be anything there that Annabel would want. Uncle
Nick had still been into the The Who and groups like
that – way back, not their kind of music at all. He
looked across the room at Annabel. She was very
pale. She kept taking things out of drawers and
putting them back in. As Simon stared at her she
caught his eye. "I don't really *want* any of these
things," she said defiantly. "It feels like stealing."

"He was your uncle. He wouldn't have minded,
would he?"

"I don't know."

"What will happen to it all if you don't have it?"

"I told you, it'll go to the dealers."

Simon crossed the room and stood beside her. "You could use things like this at school," he said, picking up a roll of sellotape. "It'd be silly not to take things you could use."

Annabel still looked uneasy. "I suppose you're right," she said, "but you see, Uncle Nick wasn't . . ."

"Wasn't what?"

"Oh, nothing. Never mind."

"I still think you ought to have a good look at all this stuff. There might be something valuable here."

"There isn't. Mum came over straight after the funeral. She was afraid there might be break-in. You know what people are like around here. It wouldn't be anything to them that Uncle Nick had just died. All they'd care about was that the flat was empty and there might be something to . . ." She stopped and bit her lip. She had been going to say "nick". It was the sort of pun that under any other circumstances they would all have laughed at. Now it wasn't funny at all. ". . . to steal," she said. "Anyhow, Mum took the things that were of any value – not that he had much. He never spent much money on things for the home. He was hardly ever here, anyway – only to sleep. He was at work all week, he had most of his meals out, and every weekend he used to go away, Friday night to Sunday night."

Simon was hardly listening. He was interested in something else. "I wonder why he had all these Ordnance Survey maps?" he asked. "He could practically cover the whole of the British Isles with this lot. I wish . . ." He stopped himself just in time.

Annabel noticed, and understood, the flush that came over his face. Simon was keen to become a surveyor and she knew how he loved maps. She knew he had been going to say how he would love to have all these. She said, "Take them if they're any good to you. You might as well. I don't want them."

"I would like them, but it doesn't seem right to take them all."

"Why not? You can get them into your school bag, can't you? Oh, Simon!" she snapped, rather impatiently. "Take them if they're any good to you, for heaven's sake! I want to get out of here." Hastily she stuffed a few useful things into her own bag – pens and paper clips, a ruler and set square – and turned to look at Julie, who was completely absorbed in a book she had taken from a shelf. Julie was a great reader. She would read the regulations on a train ticket if there was nothing else. "If you want that book," Annabel said, "take it."

Julie looked up. "I didn't know your uncle was interested in ornithology," she said. "Look at all these books about birds. This one is a beauty, full of illustrations and colour plates. It cost fourteen ninety-five. And this one – this is all birds' eggs and nests. And this . . ."

"I told you you could have as many as you want," Annabel said. "Only do hurry."

"Thanks, Annabel. I'll take good care of them, just in case you ever want them back." Julie selected some of the best and hugged them against her chest. She'd have a lovely long read in bed tonight. And her little brother Tim would be ever so pleased about them, too. He'd curl up with her for ages as long as she read to him, whatever the book was.

They were going out of the room when suddenly the telephone rang. The shrill note was like a scream in the atmosphere of the dead man's home. The three friends stood rooted to the spot. They stared at the instrument on the table as if it had some evil intent towards them. After a few moments Simon said, "Aren't you going to answer it, Bel?"

"I couldn't. I really couldn't, Simon."

The ringing continued. "Well, do we leave it or do we answer it?" said Simon.

"You answer it."

He picked up the receiver. "Yes?" he said, and then, "No – he isn't. No, he won't be back." He listened for a moment longer, then slammed down the receiver. His eyes met Annabel's. "Come on, let's go!" he said.

"Was it somebody wanting Uncle Nick? Tell me, Simon."

"Yes, it was. And he wasn't very polite, otherwise I'd have told him what had happened."

"Well, whoever he is, he'll find out about Uncle Nick sooner or later. Let's go home."

It was growing quite dark. Annabel was glad she had asked Simon to go with them. It wouldn't have been pleasant for two girls on their own. She could see that Julie was really scared. It had been the phone call, of course – it had unnerved them all.

"Let me help you with some of those," she said,

taking two of the larger volumes from Julie's arms. She was afraid that if her friend trembled much more she would drop them all in the dirty rainwater that had gathered in the yard. Julie stopped for a moment to cram one of the smaller books into her bag. A cold wind had sprung up since they entered the flat, and the dampness would soon turn to drizzle. All three of them suddenly felt that they wanted to be in a warm, cheerful room with their own possessions around them and their kind of music on the record player. They began to hurry.

The man in the raincoat waited until they had turned the corner, then followed at a distance. Just one of them he could have tackled, but three would be too many. He kept them in view all the way to the close where they lived, watched the boy go into one house, and waited for the girls to split up. They stood talking for a moment on the pavement, but he was too far away to hear what they were saying.

Annabel said, "Russell's car's in our drive. Do you mind if I come in with you for a while?"

"No, I don't mind," Julie said, "but you'd better give your mum a ring when you get in, otherwise she'll worry." She paused for a moment, then went on, "I thought you said that Russell was okay?"

"He is, but I still feel a bit awkward when he's around. It isn't the same as having Dad in the house. Mum understands how I feel. She thinks it'll be better when they're married – maybe it will. I don't want to spoil it for Mum. She's still attractive and she's been a widow for over two years. I do try not to be jealous of Russell. He's a very nice man." They went into Julie's house and closed the door. It hadn't occurred to either of them to glance back the way they had come, but even if they had they wouldn't have taken much notice of the man who suddenly turned on his heel and went to find the nearest telephone box.

He had to ask for further instructions.

Chapter Two

The following day Julie was late home from school. Mrs Briers didn't start worrying until half past five, but at six o'clock she was becoming quite anxious. It wasn't like Julie to be delayed and not to let her know where she was. She went to the phone and dialled Annabel's number. Mrs Pedrick answered. "Has Julie come home with Annabel?" asked Mrs Briers.

"No. Annabel had a dental appointment at three-thirty, so I met her and we came straight home afterwards. It didn't seem worthwhile going back to school just for twenty minutes. Why? Hasn't Julie arrived yet?"

"No."

"Have you asked Simon? She may have gone in with him."

"I'll try, but I'm sure she would have phoned me if she had. She knows how I worry."

"Well, let me know if she's not there, and I'll get the car out and cruise round a bit. Something may have happened to delay her at school. Try not to worry. Remember the time Annabel twisted her ankle and it took over an hour for her to hobble home. It could be something like that."

"I do hope so." She dialled Simon's number. "Simon," she said, "is Julie there?"

"No, Mrs Briers, I haven't seen her." He went on to explain that he had been helping a teacher with a project his form was working on. When he had come out of school there had been no sign of the girls and he had assumed that they had got tired of waiting and had walked home together. He hadn't seen Julie since lunch-time.

When Mr Briers came home from work he immediately phoned Mr Davidson, the headmaster, to enquire if any pupils had stayed late at school. Mr Davidson said he would contact some of the teachers to ask if there had been any reason for Julie to be delayed. In the meantime, he suggested, it would do no harm if Mr Briers contacted the police.

Not knowing Julie's fine sense of responsibility, the police were inclined to think that she had gone home with one of her school friends and had simply forgotten to let her parents know. "She wouldn't do that," Mr Briers retorted, somewhat angrily. "She knows how her mother worries about her. And she knows the dangers. If she had gone home with

11

anybody she would have found some way of letting us know."

"All right, sir. Give me a description of your daughter and we'll see what we can do."

Mr Briers put down the phone. "I don't think they're taking it seriously enough," he said. "They seem to think she'll turn up safe and sound. I suppose they get these calls all the time, and let's face it, there are some youngsters who don't care whether their parents worry or not."

"And some parents," replied Mrs Briers sadly, "who don't care too much where their children are."

Mrs Pedrick and Annabel came to the door. They had been driving around for an hour. They had gone to the homes of all the friends Annabel could think of, but nobody had seen Julie. Two of them remembered her waiting at the school gates, and one of them had told her that Annabel had a dental appointment, but none of them had seen her after that.

When Mr Briers had said he didn't think the police were taking it seriously enough he did them an injustice. By this time the name of Julie Ann Briers had been tapped into police computers all over the county, and within a few minutes of Annabel and her mother leaving the house, a police officer arrived. He asked a lot of questions which seemed irrelevant: what were Julie's interests? Where did she go on Saturdays and Sundays? Did she have a regular boyfriend? Did she look older than she was? He went upstairs into Julie's room. Were there any clothes missing? Did she have a savings books and if so, where was it kept? Had she taken any cash from the house? It was only then that the Briers realised that the police knew exactly what they were doing. They were checking up on the possibility that Julie had run away from home and that she might have been planning it for a long time. There was no point in being indignant, it was no use telling the officer that Julie was extremely happy at home and that they were a close, loving family. He was only doing his job. He consoled them by assuring them that Julie's description had been given to every policeman on the beat and that her whereabouts could come in at any moment.

But the minutes ticked by, and then the hours. Julie's little brother had been put to bed, crying for his sister. Mrs Briers was white and distraught. She knew now that something was terribly wrong. Julie would never stay away so long unless she had been forcibly restrained. She began to cry, quietly and hopelessly.

At midnight the telephone rang. So many people had called asking if they could do anything or to express their concern, that Mr Briers spoke into the instrument rather sharply. People were kind, but why didn't they realise that every time the telephone rang their hearts turned right over? Why didn't they keep off the line, for heaven's sake, in case there was a really important call? As it happened, this *was* an important call.

"Mr Briers?" said the voice. "Mr Peter Briers?"

"Yes."

"I've got your daughter here."

"You've got Julie? Where is she? Is she all right?" He put his arm around his wife's shoulders.

"She's very distressed, I'm afraid, but she hasn't been harmed."

"Let me speak to her."

There were confused murmurs, footsteps in the background, and then Julie's voice. "Dad? Oh, Dad!"

"Julie, where are you? Who are these people? What do they want?"

"They don't want anything. Please come and fetch me home. I want to come home."

Mrs Briers grabbed the receiver from her husband's hand. "Are you all right, Julie? Where are you?"

"I'm at – oh, I don't know. Just a moment."

A woman's voice spoke. "We're at Tendale Farm on the Hildenbury Road. Can you come over?"

"Oh yes – yes!" cried Mrs Briers. "We'll come at once!" And she put down the receiver.

Mr Briers stared at her in horror. "You shouldn't have done that," he said.

"Why not? Come on, Peter, let's hurry!"

"Look, Tess, try and calm down. First of all we've got to let the police know that we've heard from her. And we've got to get somebody to stay with Tim while we're out. I'll get in touch with the police – you get hold of one of the neighbours to come and sit with Tim."

Mrs Briers, who in her anxiety would have jumped straight into the car without stopping to think of

14

anything but seeing her daughter as soon possible, had to contain her impatience long enough to run across to Annabel's house. She found Annabel and her mother sitting up waiting to see if they could be of help. Both of them returned with her.

"What did the police say?" she asked as they set off in the direction of Hildenbury.

"They'll be there before us."

"Is that all they said?"

"That's all."

"They didn't say who lived at the farm?'

"No, just that they would meet us there."

Tendale Farm was tucked away along a track and difficult to spot from the main road. They drove past it twice before Mrs Briers detected lights at some distance. "There – there!" she cried. "That's the police car flashing, isn't it?"

A constable was waiting for them. "Your daughter's fine. No need to worry," he said. "Go straight in."

Julie ran into her mother's arms. There were two other police officers there, a man and a woman. An elderly, homely woman, who introduced herself as Mrs Fletcher, came out of the kitchen bearing cups of coffee. "Sit down," she smiled at them. "You look as if you need this."

"No, thank you," Mrs Briers said. "We'd rather go home. It's very kind, all the same."

Mrs Fletcher bent down and whispered, "I don't think you'll be allowed to go just yet. Julie hasn't finished telling the lady constable what happened."

"But we want to take her home! She looks exhausted and terrified."

"Yes, but they have to check, you see. They have to check that we – that is my daughter and son-in-law and I – are telling the truth. They want to know how Julie came to be here. You do see that, don't you? You do understand that they have to know whether or not we harmed her?"

"Yes, I see." Mrs Briers accepted the mug of coffee, which was hot and sweet, and which she had to admit she needed, for she had tasted nothing since lunchtime that day.

The woman police constable asked Julie if she minded other people being in the room while she told her story. "If there's anything – anything at all you feel shy about, we'll go into the other room. I'm unshockable, love. You can tell me anything."

Julie said she wanted to remain where she was. There wasn't very much to tell. She hadn't been hurt or molested in any way.

She had waited for Simon at the school gates. She knew that Annabel had a dental appointment. But Simon hadn't turned up, so she had started to walk home alone. As she passed the entrance to the school playing fields it occurred to her that he might have a late practice match – he was a star member of the football team and had been talking about an important match to be played next Saturday.

It was a stupid thing to do, she said, she realised that now, but she had walked a little way up the footpath towards the playing fields just to see if there was any sign of the team. By that time dusk was falling, though it was by no means dark. Hearing no sound of voices, she had turned to retrace her steps when she saw a man coming towards her from the direction of the road. There was something about the way he stopped right in the middle of the footpath that frightened her, so she turned and ran. She was a good runner, being the Inter-Schools 400m champion. She thought the man was somewhere in his thirties. Had he been younger and fitter he might have been a match for her, but as it was, she began to outdistance him as he pelted after her across the playing fields. "You just don't think at a time like that," she said. "It was stupid of me to run to the top end of the football pitch – I could have turned towards the backs of the houses and got over a wall, or screamed my head off, or something, but I just didn't think. I was too scared. Then I realised that there was only the railway ahead of me, with a fence and a hedge, and I just panicked."

By a stroke of luck she had run towards a gap in the hedge, where children must have made a path through to the railway line. "I don't know if the man was too big to get through the gap," she said. "I turned towards him just when I got there and threw my school bag at him. It hit him on the side of the head and he cursed. I got through the gap and ran down the embankment."

She hadn't heard him coming after her. She had run across the track. As she reached the other side a train came along, and while it was passing she spotted

17

a railwayman's hut close by. She opened the door and went inside. It was still light enough to see that there were some iron bars stored inside the hut. She jammed one of these under the door to prevent it being opened from the outside, then waited. There was a small window in the hut, covered over with a metal grid. She peeped out but couldn't see anybody. She sat down on the floor and waited again. Lots of trains went by, but she had no watch and had no idea how much time passed before she looked out of the window again. She saw that it was very foggy. There were fewer trains and she realised that the rush hour had long since gone.

Her idea was that she should wait there until morning, when the railmen might come and help her; but then she thought of her parents and how anxious they must be, and knew she had to get out. Even so, she waited a little longer before cautiously removing the wedge from under the door. Inch by inch she opened the door, until she could lean out and look around. Unless the man was hiding on the oppositie side to the door, there was no sign of him. She had to risk it. She didn't dare go back the way she had come, and the only alternative was to take to the open countryside on the other side of the track from the playing fields. "People who talk about being scared to death," she said, "don't know what it means. Running in a race makes your heart beat fast, but I've never known mine thump the way it did then. If I'd seen the man then I think I should have died of fright, but it was bad enough tearing through all that rough land, what with the fog and everything. I heard some terrible screams and I just dropped down on my knees and prayed. I don't know what they were, but it sounded like evil spirits. It was horrible!"

"Foxes," said Mrs Fletcher.

"What?"

"Foxes. If you've never heard them before and don't know what it is to hear them at this time of the year, you might well believe they were evil spirits. Oh, I know they look like cuddly little dogs, but in spring they can utter some blood-curdling shrieks. We're quite used to them here. Quarrelling over their mates, you see."

Julie had never before been in open countryside at night. The fog made it difficult to follow a straight course and she must have wandered in circles. There were no lights, no stars visible. Had it been a clear, moonlit night she would have seen the lights of the farmhouse in the distance. As it was, she wandered about for so long that it was past eleven before she found her way to the house. She sat on a bench in the yard, trembling, afraid to knock on the door in case she found the occupants unfriendly. Then she had noticed a small pair of red wellies in the porch, and reckoned that anybody with a small child must have compassion, so she had knocked. And that was all.

The police seemed satisfied, but she would have to make a full statement when they called at her house. Would she try, in the meantime, to remember anything she could about the man who had pursued her? They would go and search the area as soon as it was light. Yes, they said in answer to her query, they would look for her school bag and return it to her. As she said it contained nothing of value, it was unlikely that the man had taken it with him.

Nobody connected the incident with the death of Nick Lestor. After all, there was absolutely no reason why anybody should.

Chapter Three

The same night that Julie had been chased by the stranger, somebody broke into Nick Lestor's flat. "Is anything missing?' was the first question the police asked Mrs Pedrick.

"There was nothing worth taking. I cleared out everything of value, and when I offered what was left to the dealers they quoted such a low price for it that I didn't think it was worth accepting, so I asked the PDSA to take it away." She looked around at the disorderly mess: drawers had been emptied in the middle of the room, cupboards gaped open, their contents scattered and trampled on, books had been swept off the shelves, and records torn out of their sleeves.

"Looks like kids," said the constable who had

come in response to a phonecall. "There's a lot of this sort of thing going on around here – just vandalism, boredom. How long has the flat been empty?"

"Just over a fortnight." She explained the position, and the constable shook his head.

"I'm surprised it wasn't done before now," he said. "A place empty for that length of time doesn't stand a chance. I suppose in a way you're lucky that they didn't throw ink and paint around. You should have seen what they did to the infants' classroom at the local school a couple of months ago. It's going to cost a pretty penny to put that right, I can tell you." He made notes in his book and said they would look into it, but Mrs Pedrick told him it was hardly worth wasting time on the case. She said she was due to hand over the key to the new tenants in a couple of days' time, and that would be the end of it. She didn't want anything more to do with the place.

When the policeman had gone, Annabel said, "I don't understand why they did it."

"The constable told us, love. Just the sheer pleasure of doing wanton damage. I wish I knew who their parents were. I'd give them a piece of my mind."

"No, but if it was kids, why didn't they take things like this?" She picked up a box of felt-tip pens and a roll of tape. "Just the sort of things that kids would stuff into their pockets. So why didn't they? And this –" turning to a magnifying glass – "this is worth taking, isn't it?"

"I don't know. Maybe they were interrupted and

ran away. Who knows?" Annabel wandered aimlessly about the room and then followed her mother into the kitchen. "Mum," she said thoughtfully.

"Yes?" Mrs Pedrick was putting a few cans of food into her bag. "Might as well take these, I suppose."

"I – I don't feel comfortable here."

"I know how you feel. Neither do I. We'll go when I've done this."

"What I mean is, I feel awful about saying it, but I – I never really liked Uncle Nick." She had got it off her chest at last and waited for her mother's response with apprehension.

Her mother turned and faced her. "I didn't think you did," she said calmly. "The truth was, there were times when I didn't care much for him myself. We weren't brought up together, you know."

"I thought you'd be annoyed with me for saying it. After all, he *is* dead, and it doesn't seem right to talk about a dead person in that way."

Mrs Pedrick attempted to make a joke of it. "Well, I suppose people don't become angels just because they've left this world. Nick had his bad points – in many ways he was very hard." She paused for a moment and then went on, "He was my half-brother. We had the same father, different mothers. My mother died soon after I was born, and Dad married again. I liked my stepmother well enough, but she and Dad were killed in an accident when they were on holiday. That was when Nick and I were separated. He was only three. He went to one side of the family and I went to the other. I hardly saw him for the next twenty years, and even when I did I couldn't feel anything for him. He was brought up to be very hard, you see, and I'm just the opposite."

"I know you are, Mum. Soft as a brush!"

They threw their arms around each other. "We've had some bad luck, haven't we, love?" Mrs Pedrick said. "First your dad and now all this. But it's over now and we must make a fresh start. You don't mind about Russell, do you? He's a very good man, you know."

"Of course I don't mind. It'll just take a bit of getting used to, that's all – when you're married."

Annabel's father had died two years ago, from a rare virus. For a time they were both inconsolable, but gradually the hurt had healed. Mrs Pedrick had met Russell Barnes and they were to be married in two weeks' time. They were going to Wales straight after the wedding at the register office, to pick up Nick's car, which was in police care near the place where Nick had been killed. While they were away, Annabel was going to stay with Julie's family.

Annabel got on quite well with Russell. He treated her like an adult, which she liked, but she had a strange feeling that neither she nor her mother knew enough about him. He said he worked for an insurance company, investigating claims or something – Annabel didn't really understand about insurance – and he was away rather a lot. She supposed her mother didn't mind that – at any rate, she had never made a fuss about it, and it was her business more than Annabel's.

They locked up the flat for the last time, deposited the key at the Council offices, and went to buy a box of chocolates for Julie. They found her being thoroughly spoiled. She had had breakfast in bed. Her father had gone out early and bought her a tracksuit she had admired in a shop window earlier in the week. The headmaster and his wife had called and brought her a huge bunch of flowers. There had been lots of calls from well-wishers – and the curious.

She grinned a little self-consciously when her new visitors arrived. "I'm all right, you know," she said. "I'm not an invalid. Last night I was scared out of my wits and crying like a baby, but I'm over it now and I just feel mad – really mad – that anybody should go for me like that."

"Well, if I were you I'd be lapping up all this attention," Annabel said. "I'm sure I shouldn't have been half as brave as you were."

"You were very lucky it all ended without harm," Mrs Pedrick put in. "I shouldn't be surprised if you had nightmares about it for the rest of your life."

"I didn't dream at all, as it happened. And when I woke up this morning, my first thought was that it was a pity nobody timed me as I ran across that field. I must have exceeded my personal best by about fifteen seconds!"

"Well, now we know what to do at the next County Athletics Meeting," laughed Julie's father. "We'll get somebody to scare you just as the gun goes off!"

"Such as?" said Julie. "Putting a man in a trenchcoat in the next lane?"

25

Annabel stiffened. "Is that what he was wearing?" she asked. "A trenchcoat – one of those with tabs on the shoulders?"

"That's right – that's what the policeman called it when he took my statement this morning. He seemed to think that was why the man didn't catch me – the coat slowed him down. No credit to my athletic talent!"

"But I saw that man!" cried Annabel. "He was outside the school gates when I went for my dental appointment. Didn't you notice him, Mum?"

"No, I always have to concentrate on my driving when I'm pulling out of the school gates. Why didn't you mention it at the time?"

"There was no reason to. He was just a man standing on the pavement. I didn't know he was waiting for Julie to come out."

"Waiting for Julie!" echoed Mrs Briers with a little shudder.

"Well, for anybody – a girl on her own. You know what I mean."

"Mr Davidson's going to make an announcement about it on Monday at assembly," Julie said. "Warning everybody, you know. I made him promise not to mention my name, just to say that an attempt had been made to – what's the word, Dad? What the policeman said."

"Abduct."

"To abduct one of the girls at the school. My life'd be a misery if everybody knew it was me."

"I won't tell," promised Annabel. "You'd better warn Simon not to, either."

"I've already threatened what I'll do if he breathes a word. He came over first thing this morning, and he promised."

During the weekend Annabel kept thinking about the man in the trenchcoat. If she had come out of the school gates on her own when she went for her dental appointment, would he have attempted to abduct her? Surely it couldn't have been that he was waiting for Julie, and only Julie? There was something about it that made her feel cold, the same sort of feeling she had had ever since Uncle Nick died, though why the two things should be connected in her mind she didn't know.

On the following Monday afternoon Julie was a little late coming out of school. "You're late!" Annabel said. "We were getting worried."

"Don't *you* start! Mum's bad enough. She's been watching me like a hawk all weekend, and I'll bet she'll be waiting at the window when I get back. Dad had to talk her out of taking me to school and fetching me back, just as if I were a baby."

"You can't blame her," said Annabel.

"Anyway," said Simon, "what kept you?"

"Oh, I had to go and see Mrs Atkinson about the school books that were in my bag, and there was some work I should have handed in . . . I didn't see why I should have to do it all over again."

"Didn't the police find your school bag, then?"

"No. Would you believe it? That creep must have taken it. I hope he gets some satisfaction out of my essay on the Industrial Revolution. Maybe he'll mark it and send it back to me – Nine out of ten. Could do better!"

"Why on earth should he take your bag?" said Simon. "It wasn't even leather."

Julie shrugged. "Maybe he didn't. Maybe he just left it lying around and somebody else found it first thing in the morning. But the police said they were there before seven o'clock and I can't think there'd be anybody walking on the playing fields at that time of the day. Anyway –" she held up a new canvas bag she had been carrying – "Dad went out and bought me this." She smiled. "There's one consolation: for the next few days at least I shall be able to have practically anything I ask for! And Mrs Atkinson said I needn't worry about the work and I won't have to do it again. I wish I'd known that before it happened – I hate the Industrial Revolution. It took me hours to write that essay."

As they walked home Julie began to talk to Simon about a party they'd been planning for some time. Neither of them noticed that Annabel wasn't joining in. She wasn't even listening to their chatter. Something Julie had said had sparked off a most chilling idea which she was turning over in her mind. It wasn't until they were nearly home that she spoke.

"Julie," she said impulsively, "your old school bag – was it only school stuff you had in it?"

"Oh, forget it, Bel. It was an old thing anyhow. I like this one much better."

"No, Julie, it's important," she urged. "Do you remember when we went to Uncle Nick's flat the other day and you came away with some of his books? What did you do with them?"

"I took them home. I'm reading one and the rest are on the shelf in the lounge. Why? What's it got to do with my bag?"

"Didn't you put one of them *in* your bag, just as you were coming out of the flat?"

"I don't remember."

"You did – I'm sure you did. It was a small one, that's why. It kept slipping off the top of the others you were holding, so you put it in your bag."

"Oh, yes – that was the one about eggs and nests, wasn't it? I thought Tim might be interested in it, but he liked the one about sea birds best. It has some gorgeous pictures of the coast in it . . ."

"Did you take it out?"

"What?"

"Oh, Julie, listen to me – did you take the book out of your bag?"

"I suppose so." She thought for a moment. "No, I don't think I did. Look, Bel, what are you getting at?"

Simon said, "She thinks that man who came after you was trying to get hold of the book – isn't that right, Annabel?"

"Thank goodness somebody around here can *think*! Yes, that's exactly what I'm thinking. I know it sounds far-fetched, but it would explain why he took your bag, Julie."

"Just for a bird book? He must be pretty hard up."

"But what if he thought it was something else? A diary, a notebook? It was that sort of size."

Simon was beginning to look excited. "And you think it ties up with the break-in at the flat! You think somebody was looking for a diary?"

"Well, what do you think? I've been wondering for days what it was that gave me the shivers when we went to the flat. You remember I told you I'd had the feeling I was being watched when I went on my own? I said there were people near the garages, didn't I? I didn't take much notice of them because there are always people taking a short cut through there, but then I saw that man hanging around the school gates on Friday afternoon. Why should I have remembered that? He was just a man – he could have been somebody's father waiting there." She stopped. They were already in the close where they lived. "But just now, as we were walking home, it suddenly struck me that one of the people outside the garages that day was wearing the same kind of coat."

"Are you sure?" gasped Julie.

"I can't absolutely swear to it, but I'm pretty sure. It's one of those things – you don't *see* it at the time, but it's registered like a photograph and it comes back later."

They stared at each other in dismay for a moment.

30

Simon was the first to break the silence. "What do you suppose your uncle had to hide?" he asked. "Why should he keep a notebook that was so important to somebody else that he would risk all he did to get hold of it?"

"I don't know." Annabel hesitated, still feeling guilty about her thoughts. "The truth is, there were things about Uncle Nick that puzzled me. I didn't really care for him very much."

Julie was looking across the road towards her house. "What did I tell you?" she said. "Mum's looking out for me already. Do you think we ought to tell her? Tell the police? They still haven't caught the man, and what you say might help them."

"No!" Annabel sounded so adamant that the other two gaped at her. "What do you think would happen if we made a fuss about it? There may be nothing in it, but our parents wouldn't think so. We wouldn't have a minute to ourselves – they'd always be watching us. Besides, Mum and Russell are getting married on Easter Saturday and I don't want to spoil it for them. Let's have a talk about it later on. Come over to my house when you've done your homework."

Chapter Four

The man who liked to be known as Brogden dialled a number, the first three digits of which were 010. Several bleeps, clicks and squeaks later a voice came on the line.

"Speak English," said Brogden.

"Yes, sir? The Ambassador's residence."

"Let me speak to Van Hoof."

"I regret to say he is unavailable at the moment, sir. I will connect you with the ambassador's secretary."

"This is a personal call. Tell him it's Brogden."

"Very well, sir."

As he waited, Brogden looked with satisfaction at his reflection in the hotel room mirror. A failed actor, he had an excellent knowledge of the art of disguise.

There were now sandy-coloured tints in his hair and eyebrows, and his lips were thinner in appearance than they had been that morning. He was dressed in a casual open-necked shirt and jeans, with a good-quality anorak. He had dropped the rather sloppy slouch of the past few days and the trenchcoat was travelling north in an old bus being driven by a hippy who had admired it in a sleazy cafe on the Old Northern By-way.

Brogden had turned to crime, but was still acting out the macho parts he had always longed for and never secured. It was his agent's fault, of course – never being in the right place at the right time, never keeping in touch with producers who were casting new plays. There was nothing wrong with his acting, but when his big part in the London theatre had finished he had had to turn to other things, and now he was finding that he enjoyed the excitement of his work. The police were so slow, so unbelievably stupid. He could outwit them every time. But he liked to live well, he had expensive tastes, and Van Hoof must be made to realise that his services didn't come cheap any more.

"Yes?" said the thin, rather effeminate voice over the international wire.

"These calls are expensive, Van Hoof. I hope you appreciate that."

"Of course. I have never failed to meet your expense account. What have you to report?"

"There was nothing in the flat."

"Were you seen?"

"Of course I wasn't seen. I'm good at what I do. The kid hadn't got it either."

"So what do you propose to do now?"

"I'm open to suggestions. One of the other two might have it – or the sister. She's been to the flat three or four times."

There was a light click on the line. Van Hoof said, "You will appreciate how difficult it is for me to give specific instructions over the telephone. However, you know what the position is. You must stop at nothing to prevent this information from getting out."

"Nothing?"

"You know my views."

"That comes very expensive."

"Do it."

Brogden smiled to himself. "And there's another thing. The woman is going to be married soon – to – the enemy. You understand?"

"I understand. That's unfortunate."

"It's more than that. It's impossible for me to be in two places at once. They're going to Wales to pick up the car."

"I'll send Dirk over."

"The sooner the better. But don't forget to let him know that I'm in charge, okay?"

"As you wish."

"I'll be in touch."

Brogden replaced the receiver and went into the hotel bar for a drink. As he sat alone in a corner he thought hard. It had been easy so far. Ordinary people never think of such a thing as being followed. He was sure he hadn't been noticed. When he had run after the girl she had been too scared to turn and get a good look at him. All she had got was a glimpse of the side of his head when she had flung the bag at him. His head was still slightly sore where the bag had struck him. That kid could run! Of course she must have thought he was out to molest her, but that wasn't his nature. He would have to be a bit more callous now. Somebody in that family had got hold of Nick's records, and he meant to have them.

At about the time Brogden set off for the hotel bar, Annabel was putting a tape into her player. It was of a new group, Blue Ark. Simon and Julie had joined her in the lean-to at the back of the house, which was her special 'den'. Her beloved cat, Poppers, stalked out of the room in disgust. He hated music. Her mother was going out to dinner with Russell, who was waiting for her to finish getting ready. He popped his head round the door. "How's things?" he asked cheerfully.

"Fine, thanks," Annabel replied.

"Brought you something," he said. "Catch!"

Annabel caught the box of chocolates. "Thanks, Russell."

He spoke briefly but affably to Julie and Simon, then withdrew, closing the door behind him.

"I looked on the bookshelves," Julie said, unable

to contain herself any longer. "The egg book wasn't there. I *must* have left it in my bag."

Annabel threw a glance at the door. "Don't talk about it till they've gone," she whispered.

Her mother looked in. "We're off now," she said brightly. "There's plenty to eat in the fridge and lots of snacks in the cupboard. Help yourselves."

"Thanks, Mum. Have a good time."

"I will. Bye, love!"

The front door banged shut. The sound of Russell's car came over the music. Annabel checked that the door of the lean-to was securely bolted. She went and sat down cross-legged on the old settee. "You're sure the book wasn't there?" she said eagerly. "Your dad wouldn't have taken it for any reason?"

"Good heavens, no! It's not my dad's sort of thing at all."

Annabel caught sight of Simon's face. "What are you looking so pleased about?" she demanded.

"I'm not looking pleased."

"Well – self-satisfied, then. Smug. What have you got in the carrier?"

By way of reply, Simon turned the plastic bag upside down and emptied the contents on the floor. "These," he said. They were the Ordnance Survey maps he had taken from Nick Lestor's flat.

"What about them?"

"Look. Look at this one – Dartmoor, all that area. It's marked with rings and crosses."

Julie said blankly that she didn't understand.

"Well, go on," said Annabel. "Tell us what you're

thinking. I can see you're dying to."

"It's just an idea," Simon said, not so sure of himself now that he had an audience, "but I wondered – if your uncle *was* up to something, and if that man in the trenchcoat was after something that belonged to him – do you think your uncle could have been a – spy?"

"Don't be daft!" Annabel said. "Uncle Nick wasn't brainy enough for that. He couldn't even pass 'O' levels, except one, and that was the lowest grade." She paused. "Well, maybe that was unfair. He just hated being in school, that's all. He was always skiving, Mum said. But as to knowing anything about politics and secret codes – well, it just wasn't Uncle Nick, that's all."

"Sorry," said Simon. "I said it was just an idea."

"I still don't understand about the maps," Julie said.

"I thought they might be secret meeting places," Simon mumbled. He looked a little sheepish.

"In the middle of *Dartmoor*?" Julie said.

"Well, it wasn't only there. Look at this – the Shetlands. There's a circle marked on this island – what's it called? – Fetlar. And another one here, and here." He jabbed with his finger at various points marked on the map, then looked up at the girls. "What do you think?"

"I think they were just places where he went climbing," Julie said.

It was Simon's turn to sound incredulous. "People

don't go climbing on Dartmoor!" he said. "They walk, but I don't think they climb."

"Well, he went walking then. Maybe the marks are just to show places where there's a good view, or fresh drinking water. I don't believe these maps have any connection with whatever it is the man's looking for."

Annabel, who had been studying the maps quite closely, said suddenly, "There are some circles with initials written in them. Here's one – RK. I wonder who RK was? Maybe somebody that Uncle Nick went walking with. I think he knew a Ronnie somebody. I think I heard him mention the name, somebody he worked with. But I don't know what his surname was."

"Haven't you forgotten Russell?" Simon put in. "What's his surname, by the way?"

"Barnes. It wouldn't be him. They hated the sight of each other."

"Why?" asked Julie.

"I don't know. Mum always thought it was because Uncle Nick didn't like the idea of her getting married again. I don't know why Russell didn't like Uncle Nick. All I know is that they'd never even go to the pub together, let alone walking on Dartmoor, or Wales, or Scotland."

"Was that one of the things that puzzled you about him?" Julie asked.

"Well, yes, but it was mainly that he was so secretive. He used to get really sulky if we asked him where he was going for his holidays, or what he'd been doing since we saw him last. As if it mattered!

We were all family. We told him where *we* were going and what *we'd* been doing." She paused for a few moments. "But it wasn't only that. He had a good job – well, a reasonable job, at any rate – and he never married. He had no children. He had nobody dependent on him. And yet he never seemed to have much. You'd have thought that a man in his position would have bought things like the latest video or a colour TV, but all he had was a battered old music centre and a black and white telly. I just used to think he was mean with his money, salting it all away in a bank, but after he died Mum was surprised that he had hardly any savings at all. She did wonder about that, but she's come to the conclusion that when he went away at the weekends he lived it up in posh hotels, and – and girls, you know."

Julie, who was very fair-minded, said, "Well, that was his own business, Bel, and he might have been too shy to discuss it with you. He might have had a woman companion on his walking tours."

"Yes, I suppose so. I hadn't thought of that."

"But all this doesn't explain why that creep wanted Julie's bag, or why he was hanging around outside Nick's flat – if it was the same man."

"Or why sombody broke into Uncle Nick's flat."

"Maybe it was the maps they were after," Simon suggested. He still wanted to get a little credit for spotting the symbols, and he still had a sneaking conviction that his idea about spying was a good one.

Annabel went into the kichen and came back with a tray of food and drinks. As they were eating Simon

39

had another idea. "Didn't you tell us that your mum had taken some things out of the flat soon after the funeral? Personal things? Has she still got them?"

Annabel stared at him with her mouth full of food. She chewed and swallowed. "I *couldn't* go prying in Mum's room," she said.

"Okay," Simon said, "forget it."

"But if there *is* a notebook, or a diary, about the same size as Julie's egg book," Annabel said, "it *would* look as if that's what the man was after, wouldn't it?"

Her friends nodded slowly, neither of them wishing to speak encouragement out loud. Suddenly Annabel stood up. "It's the only way we can clear up the mystery," she said, and without another word she left the room.

She was back in a few minutes, carrying a cardboard box. Her face was very white. Obviously she didn't like what she was doing. But she opened the box and moved things about. Julie noticed that her friend's hands were shaking. Then she went rigid. She looked at the others' tense faces, and took out a book. "This must be it," she said, and her voice was hardly more than a whisper.

Julie's egg book had had a makeshift brown paper cover on it. This book was bound in imitation leather. But they were the same size. From a distance they would look identical. Julie swallowed hard. "What do we do now?" she croaked.

Annabel opened the book. They all bent over it. Page after page was covered in figures and initials:

RK – 2– 4.5.84. 300, was an example, though some of the initials were single – R, C, O, and others. They studied the columns for a long time, but the only entries that made sense were the dates, in the third column.

"We might be making a terrible mistake, you know," Julie said. "All this could have a perfectly innocent explanation."

"Such as?" Simon asked. He still wanted to be proved right about his spying theory.

"Well, he might have been running a sweepstake at work, or taking bets on horse-racing."

"I suppose so. But the fourth column could be for payments he was receiving for information." He glanced apologetically at Annabel. "He might not have had the brains to be a proper spy, but he could have been an industrial spy."

"Oh, let's not get back to the Industrial Revolution," sighed Julie.

"Why not? He worked at Fisher's. They might have been developing something revolutionary that other engineers would like to get their hands on. People do pay for that kind of information. I've heard my dad talking about it."

Annabel said slowly, ignoring Simon's theory, "You don't suppose he could have been a – *black-mailer* – do you?"

"Oh, Bel!" exclaimed Julie.

None of them spoke again for a few minutes. They were all horrified at the idea of anybody connected with Annabel being engaged in such a mean and dishonourable occupation. Annabel broke the silence. "I don't want to believe it," she said. "I know I didn't like Uncle Nick very much, but I can't believe he was as bad as that. But," she added, "that man must have wanted this book very badly to have done what he did to you, Julie."

"Well," Julie responded with typical fairness, "he didn't really do anything to me. He chased me over the playing fields, yes, but he didn't touch me."

"That was because he didn't catch you," Simon said.

"It was only my bag he was after." She shivered.

"The point is," Simon said, "that you still have the book, Bel. Do you think you ought to tell your mum what we suspect?"

"I don't know what we do suspect. It's all such a horrible mystery. Mum must have looked at the book. Maybe it made sense to her and she's just keeping quiet about it. After all, Uncle Nick is dead. There's nothing she could do about it now."

"But what if the man comes here for it?"

"I'm not going to say anything to her. I can't, not just now. She's getting married in a few days' time, and if she thought I was in any danger she'd call the whole thing off. It wouldn't be fair. Anyhow, as Julie said, if our parents thought that man was out to get us, we'd never be allowed to set foot outside the door on our own. Our lives'd be a misery. All we can do is keep our eyes open and see if we can spot him watching us again. It might be that he's given up . . ."

Simon interrupted her. "The telephone call!" he said.

"What telephone call?"

"The one that I answered in the flat that day. You remember – I said he wasn't very polite and I hung up. I'll bet it was the same man. And he didn't know then that your uncle was dead. He'll have found out the truth since then. So you may be right – he may have called the whole thing off. I vote we keep quiet."

"So do I," agreed Julie.

Annabel merely nodded.

Chapter Five

"Why did we have to get here so early?" grumbled
Dirk.

"Because the Registry Office opened at nine
o'clock," replied Brogden, "and I couldn't find out
what time the wedding was."

"It's your job to find out things like that."

"It isn't my job to get caught, and if I'd asked too
many questions somebody might have got suspicious.
Barnes doesn't know me, but he's clever enough to
put two and two together when necessary." Unable
to resist a little dig at the good-looking young man at
his side, he added without looking at him, "Anyhow,
on this job you do as I say, without asking questions."

Dirk was clearly irritated at the other man's
superior attitude. He said, "I still think you could

have got to know the time somehow. You could have gone to the flower shop and said you wanted to give the happy couple a surprise bouquet."

"I thought of that, but every risk is another potential step in the wrong direction. The girl in the flower shop might have been a friend of the bride – you never know in a small town like this."

"How did you find out about the wedding, anyhow?"

"Lestor's sister and Barnes called in at a country pub the other night. I followed them and listened to them talking to the barmaid. She asked when the wedding was to be."

Dirk sulked for a while. He was a young man who usually got his own way in things. Handsome, and charming when it suited him, he could find a very silky edge to his tongue. He had an accent which the most skilful linguist might have found difficult to define. He was of very mixed ancestry, having a Portuguese mother, an Australian father, and a South African grandmother who had brought him up in Sri Lanka. Being multilingual, he was of immense use to his doting uncle, the Ambassador in Holland. Unfortunately, his very good looks and his memorable charm rendered him of little use in the business for which the Ambassador had engaged Brogden. Brogden was a uniquely forgettable man, not handsome but not ugly either – simply nondescript. He could merge into a background and not be noticed, an egg in a basket of eggs, a sparrow in a flock. Add to this his knowledge of disguise and he was perfect for the job on hand. He had been doing it for many years and had seldom, if ever, made a serious mistake. Only his trenchcoat had given him away to the three young people from Alderley Close.

"There they are," he said.

The wedding party disappeared inside the Registry Office. Other parties on this popular wedding day milled around, some just emerging from the inner regions, and others going in. Brogden poured two cups of strong black coffee from a flask and handed one to his companion.

"Now," he said, when the other had sipped, and grimaced at the taste, "this is what you do. You take the car and follow them to the reception. You wait, and then you follow them to the railway station. They're going away by train because they're going to pick up Lestor's car and drive it back. I know that because they told the barmaid. Once they've picked up the car from the police pound, you find an opportunity of searching it. You know what it is you're looking for?" Dirk nodded. "I don't have to tell you to stay in the background."

"Why me?" asked Dirk. "Why can't you do it?"

"Because I have other things to do," said Brogden as he got out of the car. "Park the car in the station car park. I have another key. I'll pick it up later." He nodded casually and walked quickly away.

Alderley Close was practically deserted. Everybody,

it seemed, had gone to the wedding. There was a milkman delivering milk, and an old, short-sighted gardener mowing a lawn. Holding a clipboard in one hand Brogden knocked at the first door on the right-hand side of the close. Nobody came to answer. He went up the path to the next house. It was going to be easy, he thought with satisfaction, but he took no chances. He included the house where the old man was working.

"Morning!" he called cheerfully as he approached. "Anybody at home here? Double glazing."

"Eh?"

"Anybody in?"

"All out. Gone to a wedding." Brogden turned away and the old man switched on his mower again.

Brogden had established the fact that the house belonging to Lestor's sister and her daughter was at the top right-hand corner of the close. He knocked on two more doors, one of them where the boy lived, and as he waited he thought of the tedium of the past few weeks. He had gone as usual to Lestor's flat to collect the goods, but there hadn't been the prearranged signal in the window which meant it was safe to approach. Lestor had had an exaggerated sense of his own importance, but besides that he had a natural distrust of people which made him approach every situation with great caution. He had told Brogden that if the signal wasn't there he must go again – and again – until it was. On one of the succeeding days he had seen a young schoolgirl go into the flat. She hadn't stayed long, and when she had left she had hurried away, obviously nervous about being in that district on her own.

He had tried the telephone, but there had never been any reply. He was patient; he spent his days in and around the town, going to the flat at the specified time on each succeeding day, but without any luck. This sort of delay had never happened before and the only explanation he could think of was that Lestor had been scared off by something and was keeping a low profile for a while.

Then one day his regular visit coincided with the arrival of the girl, whom he knew now to be Lestor's niece. She had two friends with her, a girl and a youth. On the spur of the moment he had slipped into a nearby phone booth and dialled Lestor's number. The boy had answered. It was when the lad said Lestor wouldn't be back – something about the way he said it – that Brogden realised that Lestor must be dead. Why hadn't he checked that possiblility? That had been a mistake, and Brogden didn't like making mistakes. So he had been pretty sharp with the boy.

Returning immediately to his station behind the lock-up garages, Brogden had seen the three youngsters emerge from the flat. They were loaded up with books. Suddenly it occurred to him that if Nick Lestor were, indeed, dead, there were things in that flat which ought to be located. Van Hoof would be very grateful for that. He would pay well to keep his name out of the scandal which might follow the discovery of what Lestor had been up to. Brogden's mind worked fast. There had been a notebook which

48

Lestor had always produced when a deal was in progress. It had amused Brogden that he used to enter the details in it, as if by doing so he somehow ensured that there would be no comeback. When he saw the girl with the short blonde hair putting just such a book into her school bag, he realised that he must get it away from her. He had followed them, but there had been no opportunity to approach the girl on her own.

The following day Brogden had attempted to snatch the bag from the girl – he had never been the type to accost young women – but she had evidently had other ideas. When she actually threw the bag in his face he couldn't believe his luck. But the book had turned out to be unimportant, not the record book he was after. It was now, along with the other contents of the bag, buried deep on the council rubbish dump.

And now here he was knocking on the door of the niece's house. He glanced back casually down the close. Apart from the old man, who was working with his back to him, there was no sign of life. He slipped round the back. Inside the house, he paused and looked around. If, as he thought likely, Lestor's sister had brought his personal effects away from the flat, where would she be most likely to have put them? He prided himself that he knew the ways of women: he had had two wives, and had three sisters. Women, he thought, hid money in tea-caddies, love letters in locked bureaux, unimportant family records in bed-rooms. He went upstairs.

He opened the door on the left; it was the girl's

room. Her mother's room was opposite. When Brogden opened the door he stopped, taken aback. This room was now Barnes's room too, and he had brought his belongings here ready for sorting out when he returned from the honeymoon. They were piled high at one end of the room, in front of a long, low set of drawers. Brogden swore. He wanted to leave the place exactly as he found it. Even if he had to take away some of Lestor's papers, he thought it would be some time before they were missed. But now he might have to move all those boxes before he could get at the drawers. That would take time, and the wedding party might come back before he had finished.

A glance at the bed left him satisfied that the bride and groom were probably not coming back before they set off for Wales – there was no suit laid out, no suitcases packed beside the bed. The woman had been married in a tweed suit, suitable for travelling, and there had been cases in the car that had taken them to the Registry Office. A photographic memory was a decided advantage in his line of work. Nevertheless, he ought to hurry. The girl might come back.

His eyes fell on the wardrobe. It might be worth checking that first. He was lucky. He found the box straight away, and as no attempt had been made to conceal it, he thought it likely that the woman hadn't found anything of concern. There was an envelope containing tax documents, another relating to DHSS matters, Lestor's birth certificate, membership cards for his union – nothing among the documents which

50

might lead in anyway to his under-cover activities. Brogden was skilful in such matters and soon discarded everything but the brown book which he knew so well. He put that in his pocket. There must have been other things somewhere, yet this box appeared to contain everything that had been carried away from Nick's flat.

It was lucky that so far Barnes hadn't got his hands on the book. By itself it was of little use but, combined with other records, it could lead to a lot of trouble. And those other things must be here somewhere, unless they were, indeed, concealed in the car in Wales. He had had to send Dirk to check on that. He'd wait until Dirk got in touch with him, then he'd have to come here again and make a thorough search. It was one of those houses which took a lot of going over – the woman and her daughter were the type that liked clutter.

He was turning to look at the boxes belonging to Barnes, when he happened to glance out of the window. The old man had stopped mowing and was leaning on a spade, looking towards the house. Maybe he wasn't as senile as Brogden had supposed, for he was evidently wondering where the double-glazing salesman had gone. Time to go.

At the gate he stopped and looked back at the house, made a note or two on his clipboard, as if he had been surveying the place then, with a cheerful nod to the old man, went on his way.

As Annabel stood on the station platform and waved off her mother and her new stepfather, she understood why her mother had wept when she had gone on a school exchange visit to Germany last year. It had annoyed her at the time. What right, she had thought, had her mum to spoil it for her? What on earth had she been crying about, anyhow? Well, now Annabel knew. Although she was looking forward to staying with Julie, she realised what it would be like if she had to stay at home alone – the solitary meals, the long nights, the wondering if everything was all right with the absent one. Yes, it was okay for the one who went away – they were having fun – but being left alone was a different matter. She was very thoughtful as she went home with the Briers.

As she got out of the car Mrs Briers said, "You *will* make yourself completely at home, won't you, Annabel? Just come and go as you please. I know you have things to do at home."

"Yes, I have to water the plants, and look at the post, and feed Poppers twice a day. I'd better do that now. Coming, Julie?" She spoke cheerfully, unwilling to let anybody know how much she was missing her mum already. That would seem horribly childish.

As the girls walked across the road towards Annabel's house they glanced at Simon's house. He had gone away for the Easter holiday with his parents. He hadn't wanted to go. They were visiting relatives he didn't particularly like, but the girls thought he was quite lucky, because the relatives lived in Cornwall. "He said he'd send us a postcard," Julie said. "I bet he forgets."

"Probably."

Annabel fumbled in her handbag (a present from Russell) for her key. As she pushed open the door she saw that the postman had been. They had hoped he would arrive before the party left for the Register Office, so they could have read out any late cards of congratulation, but it didn't matter now. Annabel found there were three. A flat parcel had also been pushed through the box – a wedding present, no doubt. Annabel had been given permission to open all the letters, so that she could read them over the phone when her mother called. Followed by Julie, she went through to the kitchen and placed the cards and the parcel on the table. She didn't notice a slight alteration in the position of the mat behind the door.

She slit open the envelopes. Two of the cards were from people she didn't know, the third from Uncle Tom. She pulled a face. Mum would be surprised to have a card from him. Uncle Tom had hardly spoken to them for years, miserable old codger! It was Uncle Tom and Aunt Alma who had brought up Uncle Nick. No wonder he had turned out unpleasant!

Aunt Alma was dead now, and Uncle Tom was in a nursing home. He was too crippled to come to Uncle Nick's funeral. She had been with her mother to see Uncle Tom in the nursing home, just after Dad had died, but he had been so rude that they had said they wouldn't go again. It was all to do with some stupid, silly quarrel between the two families. And though

Annabel's mother had had nothing to do with it, they had considered her as being 'one of the other lot' and had treated her accordingly. Annabel knew that the card was a sort of apology for not having sent flowers for Uncle Nick. She looked at the inside. It would have been bought for him by one of the nurses – he would never have chosen anything as nice as this. He had scrawled his signature and, underneath, the words, "Go and clear out Nick's rubbish. I want to sell the house." Annabel couldn't know that the postman had arrived *after* Brogden's visit. Nor, indeed, could he.

She opened the parcel. It contained a beautiful hand-embroidered tablecloth from an old friend of her mum's. She and Julie looked at it with great admiration, both wishing they had the sort of patience that was necessary for that kind of work. "I'll take it upstairs," Annabel said, "and put it with the other things. Mum wants them all in one place so she can send thank-you cards out all together."

They went upstairs. In her mother's bedroom Annabel opened one of the boxes which Brogden had mistakenly thought all belonged to Russell. She popped the tablecloth with its accompanying card on top, and closed the box.

She never knew what it was that prompted her to open her mother's wardrobe door. Maybe she wanted to touch, to smell, her mother's clothes, to reassure herself that she was coming back. And when she had opened the door there was something about the box containing Uncle Nick's things that made her want to take it out, to separate it from her mother's belongings.

She put it on the floor by the window. "Why did you do that?" Julie asked.

"I don't know. There's something horrible about it. Maybe it's the way he died, or because it's Mum's wedding day. I don't know. I just don't want it in there."

"Your mum will wonder why."

"I'll put it back before she comes home."

"Annabel," Julie said slowly, "wouldn't it be great if we could fathom out what the figures in that notebook mean before Simon gets back? Do you ever get the feeling that sometimes he thinks – well – that we're only *girls*? That we're not as brainy as he is?"

"We're not. At least, *I'm* not. It's got nothing to do with being a girl. Look at Louise Finchley. She's got more brain than the whole of Simon's class put together. And you're brainier than I am. I don't care about that. Simon's okay."

"I know he is. I'm not knocking him. But if we fathomed it out before he got back, he might know what to do. Come on, Bel, we've got nothing better to do."

"Oh, all right." She went to the box. When she turned around her face was very pale. "It's gone," she said, almost in a whisper.

"Oh well, never mind. Your mum must have taken it with her for some reason. Maybe it had something to do with the car."

"I do wish Simon was here."

"Or Russell," said Julie.

"I didn't know you liked Russell that much."

"No, I meant maybe Russell's taken the book."

'Whatever for? He's got no right to . . ." She broke off. He had every right now to do as he liked in their house. The thought made her feel uncomfortable. She remembered that Russell had known Uncle Nick before he had known her mother. What was it that connected them, disliking each other as they had? Was Russell somehow involved in whatever it was that Uncle Nick had been doing? "I feel sick," she said.

"You shouldn't have had that glass of champagne."

"It's not that. I'm thinking about Russell. What if he's not as honest – as *nice* – as Mum thinks he is? What if he *has* taken the book without Mum's knowledge? What if there's something really nasty involved in it, lots of money or something, and he's only married Mum to get his hands on it?" Quite unexpectedly she burst into tears.

"Don't, Bel! Please don't. We're only guessing about all this, you know, and we could be wrong."

"I don't mind about the stupid book, and I don't care about that other man. It doesn't matter now what Uncle Nick did. He's dead. All I care about is that Mum's married Russell and he may not be all that she thinks he is. I couldn't bear her to be hurt, not again."

Julie was only fourteen years old, but she knew all the feelings that Annabel had been bottling up for so long – the loss of her father, accepting a stepfather she didn't know very well, the problems about her uncle – all coming at a time when just growing up was enough to be getting on with. She took Annabel downstairs and put the kettle on. By the time it had boiled and she had made the tea, Annabel was blowing her nose and trying to smile.

"Sorry, Julie."

"What's there to be sorry about? I don't mind."

"I didn't mean to go all soppy on you."

"Oh, shut up and drink your tea!" To change the subject, Julie asked, "Who's this Uncle Tom?"

Annabel explained who Uncle Tom was, but as she spoke some disturbing thoughts were filtering into her mind. She stopped suddenly and stared into space. "What's the matter?" asked Julie.

"What?"

"You've gone into a sort of trance. Are you okay?"

"I've just thought of something. What Uncle Tom's written on the card about Nick's rubbish."

"Well?"

"Maybe it isn't all rubbish. Maybe there's something at Uncle Tom's house that would explain what Uncle Nick was up to."

"I thought you didn't want to talk about it."

"I don't really. But I am ever so worried about Mum. She thinks Russell's so kind and thoughtful and everything, but what if he isn't? I keep trying to put it out of my head, but it will keep coming back in."

"Do you know what I think?"

"What?"

"I think it'd be a good thing if we sorted it out one way or the other. I don't suppose you realise it, Bel, but you haven't been the same since your uncle died. You've been quiet and moody. We thought it was because you were so fond of him, but it isn't that at all, is it?"

"No. When he died I felt guilty because I wasn't as upset about it as I ought to have been. But how could I when I didn't really like him that much? Then I told Mum, and she said she'd never got on too well with him. And I keep thinking about Russell and Uncle Nick knowing each other before Russell met Mum. And the way they couldn't stand each other. It's hard to explain. It's just a feeling I've got."

"So we'd better do something about it. If you go on like this you'll end up really weird. Why don't you ask your Uncle Tom if he knows anything?"

"You must be joking! Me go and see Uncle Tom? Anyhow, he isn't my uncle, and we're not on speaking terms. I'm sorry about his condition – he's been in a wheelchair for years, and before he went into the nursing home he'd lived in the downstairs rooms all on his own, so it must have been pretty miserable for him. But he's a grumpy old thing. When I went with Mum to see him at the nursing home he was crazy because she suggested it might be a good idea to sell the house. Nobody was going to dictate to him what he did with his property, and even if he sold the house he was going to spend every penny on himself. Nobody from 'our lot', as he called us, was getting any of it. Mum was ever so upset."

"Where is the house?" Julie asked.

"At Scawby. It used to belong to Lord Scawby. Uncle Tom was gamekeeper. He had a bit of money left him just after he retired, so he managed to buy the house he was living in. It's right in the country."

"Well, if you've got a key I think we should go and look at it."

Chapter Six

"You're quite sure there was nothing in the car?"
Brogden asked.

"How many times do I have to say it? I'm sure."

"Barnes couldn't have taken it out before you got
there?"

"No, he couldn't. I hired a car, I followed him to
the police station, I followed him to a restaurant, and
while he was in there I searched the car. He didn't
stop anywhere else, not even at traffic lights. There's
no way he could have removed anything without my
seeing him."

"You'd better come back. I'm going to be busy.
Book in at the Belvedere Park Hotel and I'll join you
for dinner one evening."

"Which evening?"

"I don't know which evening. Does it matter? It's a comfortable hotel and you're being paid for doing nothing."

"But what am I supposed to do in a miserable little provincial town like that? There's nothing – no casino, no race-track, and the girls are all like stewed puddings. Why should I come back?"

"Because I say so. And because dear old Van Hoof would lose everything – position, power, money, everything – if the truth came out. And I'm the one who can make sure that it doesn't come out. You've done very well out of him, dear old Uncle Van, haven't you? And he's promised you that everything he has will come to you when he dies. So it's in your interest to be patient, and to trust me."

"I trust you like I trust a scorpion."

"I love you, too."

Brogden hung up. During dinner he thought carefully about the whole business. He had the book. He knew exactly what Lestor had sold, and when, but evidently he had had other customers besides Van Hoof. Who were they, and did they know about Van Hoof? And where was Lestor's address book with the names and telephone numbers of his customers? For there had to be one: he couldn't have memorised all those numbers. And the letters? It was the letters that Van Hoof was most anxious about. He could deny everything else without the letters, but with them he was lost. His signature, his special notepaper, even his fingerprints, were on those letters.

Brogden smiled broadly at the wine waiter and

ordered champagne. He didn't think that a couple of million guilders would be too much to ask for the letters. Blackmail? He preferred to think of it as a service. Van Hoof wanted the letters, Brogden himself wanted the money. Fair enough.

At ten o'clock he walked out of the hotel and turned in the direction of the girl's house. On these jobs he preferred to walk rather than use a car. By the time he arrived at Alderley Close he was in exactly the right mood for the job, confident and calm. That was important. Rush a job, get flustered, and it became dangerous.

The back door, as before, was ridiculously easy. He used a probe to manipulate and push the key out of the lock on to the mat inside, then he stretched his arm through the cat-flap and picked up the key. It was Tuesday. For two days he had sat in the car in a lane at the back of the house, watching the girl's behaviour pattern. Twice a day she had gone in, presumably to feed the cat and pick up the mail, and each time she had been back in the other girl's house before darkness fell. He saw no reason for her to do any different now. All the same, he entered quietly and stood for a moment in the kitchen. There wasn't a sound. Even the cat had gone out; he had seen it go. He placed the key back in the lock and turned it, then crossed the kitchen and went silently upstairs. In every house some light filtered through from outside, and he had no difficulty in entering the woman's bedroom and drawing the curtains before switching on his glowlight. It gave a diffused light that wouldn't be noticed from outside, but was sufficient for the job in hand.

Brogden had allowed himself half an hour. If he found nothing on the first night he would come back again – and again, if necessary. Two million guilders was worth a fair bit of trouble. He worked quickly yet methodically, but at the end of his allotted time he had turned up nothing which in any way related to Nick Lestor. He switched off his light, opened the curtains and left them exactly as they had been when he entered the bedroom. Then he went downstairs. He had to leave by the front door, which was on a latch lock, and was in the process of opening it stealthily, an inch at a time, when a thought struck him. There had been letters on the kitchen table. He paused. It was worth a quick look. He closed the front door quietly and went back.

I've got the luck of the devil, he thought as he read the card from Uncle Tom. "Go and clear out Nick's rubbish. I want to sell the house." Well, there was only one problem now – where was the house in question? How could he find out? The best source of information was undoubtedly the girl. He'd have to find some way of getting her on her own and forcing her to tell. That would mean locking her up somewhere while he went to the house, but he'd sort that out. Maybe he could take her with him, force her into the car and make her show him the way. She was shorter by fifteen centimetres than the other girl, and didn't look as athletic. She'd be easy enough to handle.

He went out of the front door, heard the lock click

behind him, and slipped round the back of the house, over the wall, and away.

In Julie's bedroom, where a camp bed had been put up for Annabel, the girls were chatting as they prepared for bed. Annabel had spoken on the phone to her mum and was convinced that for the time being, at least, she was happy in her marriage. Suddenly she said, "I've just had a thought."

"Congratulations!"

A pillow flew across the room.

"Well, what's your thought?"

"Oh, nothing much. Just that being here with you is like having a sister. You don't know what it's like to be an only child – not that I've been particularly miserable about that – but you have Tim. I just thought maybe I *shall* have a sister or a brother. Mum's still only thirty-nine. Wouldn't it be great?"

"It depends. Tim's lovely, but he can be a little beast when he feels like it."

"Yes, but it would be nice. I could take him – or her – out, and buy things, Christmas presents, birthdays, dress her up. You know." Annabel rolled over on to her back and stared at the ceiling. It didn't seem all that long ago that she had been the one who was being taken out to see Santa Claus in his fairy grotto. Mum and Dad, smiling at her, making promises to the old man in the red cloak and the false beard. Dad had been great fun – always joking, a bit noisy, a bit clumsy, but good fun. Russell wasn't a bit like him. Russell was serious and, she had to admit it, brainier than Dad had been. It was going to take a long time to get to know Russell. And then, she was always going to call him Russell, never Dad.

"What are you thinking about?" Julie asked.

"Russell."

"Do you still think he took the book?"

"I don't know."

"You still don't trust him, do you?"

"I don't know," she said again. "It's just that I think there are things he's never told us about himself."

"Well, whatever they are, maybe they're not that bad. Maybe he's told your mum and she just doesn't want you to know."

A spasm of jealousy shot through Annabel's heart. "I'm going to find out," she said, almost savagely.

"You said that yesterday, and the day before. You've got the key to your uncle's house. It's the only way to find out if Russell had any connections with Uncle Nick."

"But your mum doesn't like us to go out without knowing exactly where we're going and I understand why. She's responsible for me while I'm with you, and after that other episode it's only natural that she should worry."

"I don't think she'd mind so much if Simon was with us. But we *are* fourteen. When's she going to learn to live with it? She can't keep us locked up. Anyway, what harm can we come to going to the old man's house? There's nobody in it. Let's go, Bel! It'll be exciting, something to do."

In the morning, Julie announced, "We're going into town, Mum."

Mrs Briers controlled the expression of concern which came into her eyes. "Oh," she said brightly, "shopping?"

"Just looking around."

"I'll run you in if you like. There's a sale at Murkitt's. I'd like to have a look."

"Oh, *Mum*! We'll go on the bus. And we'll get a sandwich at The Parrot House so you won't have to bother about lunch for us."

"Do be careful, won't you?"

"Of course we'll be careful. Don't *worry*!"

"Wait until you're a mum."

Julie ignored that and shot a glance full of meaning at Annabel, who looked slightly uncomfortable and felt that she almost blushed.

"Boys!" Mrs Briers was thinking. "It's got to be. They're meeting some boys and they don't want me to know. Well, I did the same thing myself when I was fourteen – I can't stop them. It's all in the course of nature." She thought she was being very understanding, but at the same time couldn't help thinking that life was far more fraught with danger than it had ever been in her young days.

She watched them go across to Annabel's house, and a little later saw them set off in the direction of town. Annabel was a pretty girl, a very pretty girl, and Julie was attractive, too. It wasn't fair to be jealous of their youth and the fact that boys must be looking at them with favour nowadays. She sighed, and got on with her housework. She had only vaguely noticed the man reading his newspaper on the seat near the bus stop, and when she tried to recall his appearance a day or two later there was nothing at all she could remember. He was just a man reading a newspaper.

Today Brogden was wearing jeans, a threadbare brown sweater, and a light nylon jacket. He had no moustache and had discarded the glasses he had been wearing yesterday. He always cast his own roles. Yesterday he had been an electrical engineer; today he was a plumber. He felt like a plumber – he could smell putty in his nostrils. His drama training was second nature to him and he could slip into any personality he chose. The girls wouldn't recognise him any more than they had recognised him for the past three days.

He was right. They didn't glance at him. And when he took the seat directly behind them on the bus they didn't even bother to speak in whispers. Not that they talked loud – he had to concentrate hard on what they were saying, so he leant his elbow on the sill and his head against his hand and pretended to doze.

They were going to town. Their conversation was at first about the tall girl's mother. Apparently she hadn't been keen on them coming out on their own.

Presumably she was still worrying about the afternoon when he had chased the girl across the playing fields. She was the one he had to get rid of, somehow. It was the other one he wanted – Lestor's niece. She was the one who could tell him where the house was.

They started talking about the parrot house. He didn't know there was a zoo around here, but if there was, it might be a good place to separate them. He started to think of ways of inducing the girl to go with him. His casual clothes were all wrong for posing as a policeman with an urgent message from the girl's mother, but they were right for a threat. He could say he had an accomplice holding the tall girl's kid brother, he would allow *her* to run off, and Lestor's niece would be easy to deal with. As he filled in the details of his plan he heard a sudden turn in the conversation.

"Let's go to the house first."

At first Brogden thought they were still talking about the parrot house, but then he stiffened.

"You did bring the keys, didn't you?"

"Yes."

"And you're not going to chicken out again like you did yesterday?"

"I didn't chicken out. It's just that I don't like doing all this behind Mum's back, and I'm not sure about finding out what Uncle Nick was up to." Brogden felt his stomach muscles tighten into a hard knot. It wasn't possible, it *couldn't* be possible that these young kids had caught on to the truth. He leaned forward, holding his breath. "And then

68

there's Russell," the girl went on. "It'd break Mum's heart if he turned out be a crook or something, and especially if it was through me that she found out about him."

"We don't have to tell her. We can just have a look, and if we find out that it wasn't anything really bad after all, we can keep it to ourselves, can't we?"

"I suppose so."

"Oh, let's do it, Bel. I'm bored with just mooching around town. Anyway, if I thought it was going to do anybody any harm, I wouldn't go, but I don't see how it can. You know I wouldn't upset your mum any more than I'd upset mine. I know how they worry about us, but after all, what are we going to do? Just look at your Uncle Tom's house. I don't see that there's anything wrong in that. To tell you the truth, I think we're just playing games. Your Uncle Nick wasn't a scientist, he wasn't a politician, he wasn't *anything*. I'm sure we shan't find anything in the house, but at least it's something to do."

"All right, but I shall tell Mum we've been when she rings up tonight."

"Will she mind?"

"No, I don't think so."

"There you are then."

The bus pulled into the bus station. As Brogden followed them to the stand where the Scawby bus stood empty, he thought quickly. It wouldn't do to follow them straight into the empty bus. These kids were brighter than he'd thought. He went over to the office and asked what time the Scawby bus left. Then he glanced at his watch. Seven minutes to wait. He went into the shabby café and bought a cup of coffee. The girls had climbed into the bus and were sitting near the front, talking without much animation. It looked as if Lestor's niece had given up the argument.

They didn't know the truth, only that Lestor had been doing something that in their innocence they believed to be wrong. Soon they'd be grown up and then they'd accept that they had to turn a blind eye to such things. He would follow and find out where the house was, and with any luck discover the rest of Lestor's records, the letters from Van Hoof, and anything else that might lead to his own dealings with the dead man. Yet he was uneasy. If the girls went into the house on their own, they might be able to put two and two together. He didn't know what Russell Barnes might have told them about himself; if they knew what his occupation had been for the past fifteen years they must be able to add it all up.

As he watched two young mothers with three children board the bus, followed by an elderly couple, he realised that he couldn't allow the girls to go into the house. But how to stop them? And if he did manage to dissuade them somehow from going in – pretend to have gone there about a gas leak, for instance – they would still go home with the knowledge that something was wrong. They would still be able to tell their story to their parents or to the police. The police wouldn't attach much importance to it, but Barnes certainly would, and Barnes had always been a force to be reckoned with.

Three minutes to go. The bus was filling up. He finished his coffee and walked to the bus. The girls didn't seem to notice him. He sat on the opposite side of the gangway and read a newspaper which somebody had left on the table in the café. He couldn't hear what the girls were saying, but it didn't matter now. He had about half an hour (if they were going all the way to the terminus) in which to think of a way of keeping them out of the house, or at least to stop them searching. Maybe that would be the best thing. Let them go into the house and then call at the door on some excuse and get them to leave before they found anything. He could get in there immediately after they left. It was likely, from the message on the card, that Lestor's things were all in one place. "Nick's rubbish." It shouldn't be hard to locate.

So far, so good. He bit hard on a fingernail. He hadn't done that since he was in school. Stupid, getting into a state of tension through a couple of kids like that. And where was the boy? They hadn't mentioned him. What if he knew more than they did? He was a cut above the girls. When he had slammed down the telephone on his call, Brogden had felt the anger in the kid's voice. But with any luck, it would be too late for him to do anything about it. Once the letters had been located he'd be on his way.

Carelessly he dropped the paper on to his knee and it slipped to the floor. Once again, it was Barnes who bothered him. It was all very well to remove everything that could lead to Van Hoof and himself, but what about all the others who were in the game? How many of them had passed their merchandise through Lestor? How many of them knew where it was going? Some of them might. And that information might be in the house.

Brogden came as near to panicking as he had ever come in his life. He wasn't a killer. He couldn't dispose of two innocent young kids. But he had to keep them quiet for at least three or four days to allow Dirk and himself to get well clear and check up on what they knew and, most important of all, to get his money cleared and secured. Once that was done, he would make for South America, and that would be the end of Brogden. He would become Denys Jones or Michael Browne, maybe give himself a title – The Honourable, or Major, Doctor, perhaps. He was looking forward to it.

In the meantime, he had to lock up the girls.

Chapter Seven

When the bus reached the terminus, Brogden and the two girls were the only passengers left on board. The driver pulled into the lay-by and immediately occupied himself in lighting a cigarette. He hardly glanced at the three passengers as they alighted. It was a Pay-as-You-Enter bus and he had taken no notice of them as they had paid. He was a man who was very, very bored with his job and had far better things to think about than the faceless hundreds who travelled with him. More than that, he was a man who didn't get involved in things, and even if he had seen a bank robbery in progress he would have looked the other way and never said a word about it. So it was nothing to him that the girls went one way and the man the other. Not his business. He opened his sandwich box.

Brogden walked away from the girls, but on turning a corner he stopped, slipped into the field alongside the road, and ran back the way he had come. There were no buildings here, but on the other side of the road was a terrace of unoccupied, decaying houses. Only here and there, dotted about the surrounding countryside, were there any other homes, many of them weekend cottages bought by rich businessmen, and occupied only from Friday to Sunday. The Easter weekenders had gone, but two dogs barking at each other over a distance testified to the fact that there were some people still living in the area.

It was a triumph for Brogden. He hadn't anticipated such isolation. He kept well out of sight, tailing the girls, who seemed to have got over their slight difference of opinion and were laughing quite amiably together.

"I never knew Scawby was such a nice place," Julie said. "It's such a horrible name that I thought it was scruffy. Your uncle was lucky to live here."

"Yes, he knows that. I think that's why he stuck to the house for so long. He wanted to come back. But the matron at the nursing home said the last time we saw her that she was going to tell him quite bluntly that he couldn't possibly cope without full-time help."

"It must be awful to be old and disabled. I don't think I could bear it."

Annabel said, "The house isn't much, you know – it needs a new roof, and there's rot in the floorboards.

I don't know who'd buy it. I know I wouldn't want to live in it. It's okay in the summer, the trees and bluebells and everything, but it'd scare me to death to live here in the winter. No neighbours, no shops – ugh! There used to be people in those houses on the road back there, but they've all moved out now. I don't know why Uncle Tom stayed on here when he retired. I'd much rather have a nice modern flat in town somewhere."

"Is this it?" cried Julie as they approached along the rough track. "Oh, Bel, it's lovely!"

"What's lovely about it?"

"Oh, it's so – I don't know the word – *quaint*, I suppose. Like a story book house. And the roof doesn't look so bad. I thought it must be falling down, the way you described it."

"Well, I don't like it. It's so lonely. Do you really want to go in?"

"It'd be silly not to, now we've come so far. Here, give me the keys. I'll unlock the door."

As soon as Annabel entered the house she knew there was something different about it since she had last been there. It didn't smell so bad, for one thing, and for another, there was a new carpet in the hall and on the stairs. There were some pictures on the wall of the staircase, too, but when she went into the kitchen she thought it looked much the same as it had before. A bit of a mess. Uncle Tom had managed to get his wheelchair around the house, but he wouldn't allow anybody in to help with the housework. The social services people had tried, but he had sent them away.

Chores he could do at wheelchair level he had done, but the floor was dirty, the curtains unwashed, and the wallpaper peeling away, just as they had been when she saw it last.

"How long is it since you were here?" asked Julie.

"Two years. I came with Mum to fetch some papers that Uncle Tom wanted. We didn't stay long, just long enough to find his box with his tax records and things. It was the time that Dad was in hospital and we had other things on our minds besides Uncle Tom's problems. Mum tried to get in touch with Uncle Nick to ask him to come for the box, but he was away somewhere and hadn't told us where he was going. He never did. Mum was niggled about that. After all, Uncle Tom was nothing to her and she thought the least that Uncle Nick could do was to keep in touch with him." She turned abruptly and walked back into the hall.

The new carpet intrigued her. Rich ruby red, it seemed to invite her to walk on it, to follow its rosy path upstairs. It seemed the only thing in that gloomy house that was cheerful. Julie had left the door wide open, and the sunshine lit up the stairs. Why would Uncle Nick have re-carpeted the stairs instead of spending money on his own flat? She glanced into the sitting room and then the room that Uncle Tom had used as a bedroom. Both were equally shabby, both exactly as she had last seen them. "Leave the door open," she said to Julie, who had moved towards it. "Let's look upstairs."

There was a square landing with a large window.

Two bedroom doors stood open. Both were empty. A third door led to a bathroom and the fourth was closed. Annabel had never been upstairs, but she knew somehow that behind the closed door was another staircase, to the attic. She opened it and saw that the new carpet extended up the narrow stairs beyond.

On the tiny landing the girls stopped and drew in their breath. One of the two doors was open. It was just a bathroom, but totally out of keeping with the rest of the house. Everything was luxurious – pale yellow suite, gold curtains, gold-plated taps, deep yellow towels on a mahogany rail and a collection of porcelain animals on the window sill.

So this was Nick Lestor's real home, not the flat in River Street! Here he had spent his earnings on the luxury he might have had elsewhere. But why had he kept it secret? What was wrong in wanting nice things, a comfortable flat?

"This door's locked," Julie said, behind her.

Annabel turned. "Doesn't the other key on the ring fit it?"

"I haven't tried it. Do you think we should?"

"I thought you were the one who wanted to look around?"

"I do. But you never know what you might find in there."

"Who's chickening out now?"

"It's not that, Bel. You see, what if there's somebody else involved? A girl? I mean, your uncle Nick might have had a girlfriend he didn't want anybody to know about. That might be what it's all about."

Annabel hadn't thought of that. She was silent.

"If that's all it is," Julie went on, "I'm not sure that we ought to pry. It isn't our business. All we want to know is why that man chased me, and if it had any connection with the book."

"And how Russell comes into all <u>this</u>. We've come so far, Julie, I don't think we ought to go back without looking."

On the bend of the stairs Brogden went rigid. So they had worked out at least part of it! They obviously suspected that he had had some connection with Lestor, and had even tied Barnes in with it somehow. How on earth had they done it? He had been so careful. They hadn't given him a glance in the bus, so they hadn't recognised him as the same man who had chased the tall one. But there was no question about it now – he had to do something about these two. He had to take stronger measures than he had anticipated.

Turning quietly on the thick carpet Brogden went downstairs. On his way into the house he had glanced into the rooms on the ground floor. He went into one of the rooms, in which he had noticed something that was going to come in very useful.

Upstairs, the girls had ventured into the room beyond. They found it was as luxurious as the bathroom. Beautiful furniture, TV, video, good quality cabinets all along one wall, with bookshelves and cupboards. "Some rubbish!" exclaimed Julie, thinking of the words on the card.

"He wouldn't know. All this must have been done since Uncle Tom left."

"Look at this," Julie said. It was a photograph album with pictures of Nick Lestor beside a swimming pool, against a background of trees, on a golf course, sitting on a terrace. But a very different Nick Lestor from the one who had worked at Fisher's Engineering. There was a look of money about the way he was posed. All the locations were smart. There were girls there, and other men, all well dressed, all very much at ease, people who were used to the good life – and among them and equally at home was Nick Lestor. Quite clearly, he had had plenty of money.

"Oh, I don't understand," Annabel said. "I'm going to forget about it till Mum gets back. Then I'm going to tell her everything. Come on, let's go."

"Not quite yet," said a soft voice.

They spun round. In the doorway was Brogden, smiling, and in his hand was the shotgun he had found propped in the corner of Uncle Tom's bedroom.

He came into the room and kicked it shut with his heel.

He didn't want to hurt them. He had sisters of his own, and even though he didn't get on with them very well, he wouldn't have liked it if somebody had harmed them. The shotgun wasn't loaded, but the girls weren't to know that; all he wanted was to keep them quiet and still while he searched for what he wanted. "Now you *are* going to be good girls, and do as I say, aren't you?" he said softly.

They looked scared out of their wits. Neither of them spoke. The pretty one, Lestor's niece, looked as if she might faint. He liked the other one. She had guts. When he had almost cornered her in the playing fields he hadn't resented her flinging the bag at him. He would have done the same in her position. And she was superbly athletic. He stared hard at her, memorising her face. One day she would take her place on the international athletics circuit. Of course she was still very young, not more than fourteen, so it was hardly surprising that she was frightened. He said, "I want you to sit down, over there, with your backs to the wall, and don't move until I say so."

They scrambled to obey.

"Now throw the keys to me." He caught them, locked the door on the inside just in case the tall one decided to make a break for it, and pocketed the keys. Then he started his search. He worked, as always, methodically, from left to right. The first cabinet proved to be a drinks cabinet – wines, spirits, bottles of lemon and tonic water, salted peanuts, a box of chocolate mints. He tried the next – glasses, decanters, glass cloths, everything in neat order. The fourth cabinet yielded what he had come for. There were Van Hoof's letters, Lestor's address and telephone book, detailed lists of transactions, and a diary. Brogden felt elated. All he had to do now was present this evidence to Van Hoof – he thought there was a flight from the East Midlands airport late in the evening – and the money would undoubtedly be forthcoming. He turned and smiled at the girls.

"Now," he said, "I'm leaving. I shan't be coming back, but I'll send my colleague with food for you. Unfortunately, I shall have to ask you to stay here for a few days, until I have concluded some business. You won't be harmed, I can promise you that, but you might find it rather uncomfortable being cooped up here together. It's a pity, but it can't be helped. If there were any other way, believe me, I'd find it." He stuffed the documents into his plumber's bag, and just to make sure, looked into all the other cupboards. One of them proved to be a concealed washbasin. "Now isn't that lucky?" he said. "Water laid on. That will make things much more pleasant for you."

A quick glance out of the window, which looked out over rough woodland at the back of the house, and he was satisfied that there was no way the girls could escape. The window was at least twelve metres above the ground, and there was a stone terrace below it. Not even the athletic one would risk that. He went to the door, grinned, and with a final "Nice meeting you," stepped out and locked them in. It was ten minutes to two in the afternoon. He wondered if Dirk had checked in at the Belvedere yet.

Chapter Eight

"It can't have happened again!" cried Mrs Briers. "It can't!" She put her face in her hands and sobbed. She had hardly yet got over the shock of her daughter's previous disappearance, and now here she was again, pitched into the same trouble as before. It was too much to bear, especially as she was responsible for Annabel too. But what could she have done to prevent it? They weren't children any more – they were young adults, and she couldn't have locked them in their room.

WPC Williams tried to reassure her. "It's better, you know, that there are two of them. It's much more likely that they've gone off somewhere than that anything bad could have happened to them."

Mrs Briers took her hands away from her face.

"What do you mean?" she asked.

"Well, when one girl of that age goes missing, the possibility is that some character's abducted her, but two close friends points to some sort of arrangement between them – some sort of prank."

"You really think so?"

"Yes, I do."

"But what sort of prank? You mean, going off for a joy-ride somewhere?"

"Possibly, but, well, girls of that age do sometimes take it into their heads to spread their wings a bit." She wanted to avoid saying they had most likely run away from home for reasons of their own. It was surprising how even the very best, the most understanding of parents couldn't get it into their heads that their children wanted to explore the world for themselves, make their own decisions, plunge headlong into life. Not that WPC Wiliams approved of it. Such behaviour had led to some pretty nasty results in her experience, but the fact remained that young people *would* do it.

"It's not long," she went on, "since I felt the same way myself. I loved my mum and dad, but I felt choked at home. I wanted adventure, thrills. I was never wild, but I did want to do things that they disapproved of. Nothing bad, mind, but I just wasn't the prissy little girl they wanted me to be. They sent me to ballet classes and piano lessons, and all the time, from about eight years old, all I wanted was to be a policewoman. They were absolutely horrified, but in the end I got my way. Of course, I admit that when I was young I thought it was all excitement, catching baddies and locking 'em up. I know different now. It sometimes isn't a nice job at all, but I still want to do it."

Mrs Briers had stopped crying and was looking intently at the girl in front of her. "Are you saying you think my daughter – and her friend – had some secret ambition that we didn't know about?"

It wasn't exactly what Judy Williams meant, but she had had to divert the mother's mind from other possibilities. She wasn't very pleased when her colleague, Sergeant Harrison, blundered into the conversation. "You did believe her story about what happened two or three weeks ago?" he enquired.

"Believe her? Of course I believe her. She made a statement. You were there yourself. You know she was at Tendale Farm."

"But did she give an accurate account of where she was before she got there?"

Mr Briers stepped forward. "I don't like what you're suggesting," he said.

"We have to consider every aspect," the sergeant retorted.

"You think my daughter was lying?"

"I didn't say that."

Judy Williams stepped in quickly. "We do believe that Julie was happy at home, Mr Briers, and we believe that you love her and care for her, but what about the other girl? Is there anything that might have unsettled her? You said her mother had recently got married again."

The expression on Mrs Briers' face changed swiftly. "Why, yes, that's so!" she exclaimed. "Annabel's father died two years ago. We know it upset her very badly, and I don't think she was too pleased about having a stepfather. Do you think that's it? Do you think she's persuaded Julie to run away with her?"

"Some girls of that age do try to draw attention to themselves by doing things like that. It's very often a cry for help."

Mrs Briers drew in a long breath. She smiled shakily. "You could be right," she said. "They did seem to have some sort of secret between them lately. I don't know what it was. I thought it was just some silly girlish thing – you know what girls are. But there was definitely something."

"Well, we've contacted Annabel's mother and stepfather, and they're on their way home. Maybe we'll be able to piece things together when they get here. In the meantime, is there anybody else we could ask about it? Anybody the girls might have confided in?"

"There's Simon Sharp, across the road," Mr Briers said, "but he's away on holiday. The girls have always been very close to him and I doubt if they would do anything without letting him know about it."

"He's coming back tonight," Mrs Briers said. "His dad has to be back at work tomorrow."

"And in the meantime, the girls might phone you."

"You think so?"

"It does happen, I promise."

The sergeant always disapproved of the way in which Judy Williams approached these cases. He felt it was wrong to raise hopes without good foundation. If these two girls had taken it into their heads to go to London, as so many youngsters did, they might have got themselves into all sorts of trouble. Especially if they had hitched. Even two of them together would have a hard time of it with the wrong sort of lorry driver, or a car-load of pitiless men. He said, "Can you think of anywhere they might have gone to stay? Some slightly older friends in the cities? A den they might have made when they were kids? Anywhere they might have taken shelter?"

"I still don't accept your theory," Mr Briers persisted. "I don't believe that under any circumstances my daughter would do this to us. She saw how it affected us the last time she went missing. But if you want to check up on the railway hut she mentioned before, it's just possible that for some reason they're hiding there. What I mean is, that if they were in some sort of trouble, it might suggest itself to Julie as a safe place to hide."

"Yes, that's a possibility. We'll get on to it." Sergeant Harrison left.

"Try and get some rest," Judy said to the two anxious parents.

"I couldn't," Mrs Briers said. "I keep thinking that the phone will ring any minute."

But the phone remained obstinately silent, unlike last time, when anxious friends had kept the line busy for hours. This time they had told nobody but the police and Annabel's parents. Judy Williams went off duty and was replaced by a young male constable. Dawn began to break, and with it came Annabel's mother and her new stepfather.

The two houses were thoroughly searched in an attempt to find any clue that might explain the girls' disappearance or their whereabouts, but nobody could find anything that might help.

"They haven't taken anything with them," the new Mrs Barnes said. "If they had planned it, they would at least have taken a change of clothing." She looked white and distraught, for she had been travelling through the night since she had received the message at one o'clock that morning. She and Russell had been away from their hotel on a day trip to the Isle of Man, and it had been impossible to get in touch with them earlier. She placed no blame on Mrs Briers – in fact she sympathised with her. Neither she nor Russell thought of checking the box in the wardrobe that contained the dead man's personal papers. Why should a dead man's secret have any connection with the disappearance of two teenage girls?

But when Simon arrived home, things began to take on a much more sinister aspect. All the parents gathered together in the Briers' house and listened as the sergeant questioned him. The policeman was obviously amused at the boy's account of mysterious strangers and figures in a book, and the markings on the Ordnance Survey map were quite clearly, he thought, connected with the late Nick Lestor's hobby of rock-climbing. But the account strengthened the sergeant's theory that the two girls were off looking for adventure. Even the boy was hardly past the age of *Treasure Island* and all that fictitious stuff, which seldom happened in real life, and certainly not in a little town like theirs.

It was all too obviously a case of kids running away from home, and he had had his full share of that in his time. If only they realised what a waste of police time it was, when they could be better employed on real criminal cases. In fact, Sergeant Harrison was bored by the case. He was quite certain that before the day was out the girls would either have phoned or come back repentant. "I suppose they did a lot of reading?" he asked. "Adventure stories, stuff like that?"

"Oh, Julie never stopped reading," Mrs Briers said eagerly. "She was always a good reader, right from a little girl. And such a vivid imagination! Her teachers have always said that." The sergeant was now quite satisfied that his theory was right. The only worry now was that in their innocence the two girls might have been picked up by somebody on the road, but their descriptions were out and all units were on the lookout for them. He made notes and then told Simon that he could go.

Russell Barnes had listened with deep interest to what Simon had had to say. When the families split up to go to their separate homes, he said, "Simon, will you come in with us for a few minutes? I'd like to hear more about your suspicions."

"You believe me, then? I'm sure the sergeant didn't. He treated me like a kid."

"Yes, I believe you absolutely."

"Why didn't you back me up in there?"

"I have my reasons. It all ties up with something I've been working on for a long time. Admittedly, I didn't connect it with Julie's disappearance the other week, but now I think there may well be a connection. I had no idea the people involved were so desperate, but it depends on who is involved."

"You think they're desperate people, and they've got the girls?" cried Mrs Barnes. "Why didn't you tell the police?"

"I want to talk to you and Simon first."

Chapter Nine

The two girls were too shocked and frightened to move or speak until they felt absolutely certain that the man had gone. Julie was the first to get to her feet. She tried the door and then looked out of the window. "There's no way we can get out," she said.

"What can we do?"

"Try and calm ourselves first, then think. Something might occur to us."

"Who is he, Julie?"

"Well, I'm not sure, but I think he might be the man who chased me across the playing fields. There's something about his profile that looks familiar. That's all I really saw of him."

"Oh, no! Then you do think there's something in it after all? Uncle Nick, and Russell, and the book, and the maps? Oh, Julie, I do wish we'd never started all this!"

"I said I wasn't sure, but if he had no connection with your Uncle Nick, why did he take all those things away? I couldn't see what they were, but he smiled to himself when he put them in his bag, as if they were just what he'd been looking for. If your uncle used this place as a sort of hideout, those papers must have had a connection with what he was doing. Let's have a good look round. There might be something he's missed that would give us a clue."

"What's the use? I don't care what Uncle Nick was doing. I think we'd do better to try and get out of here. He said somebody else would be coming to bring us food. Let's get out of here before he comes, please, Julie!"

"I want to get out as much as you do, but we can't break down the door, and there's no other way out. The window's far too high."

"Couldn't we throw all the cushions out and jump on to them?"

"We'd break our legs even if we did that. Believe me, Bel, I did the high jump all last season and even with mats it was a hard landing. That window is three times the height I ever did. No, it's just not possible. Anyhow, I'm going to look in all the cupboards. I'm sure there might be something that will help us to understand what all this is about."

"You look. I don't care what it's all about."

"Well, I do. It might be important to us, and to your family. You don't know what's involved. If these people are so scared of us, who are they going to go for next? They might be after Simon. They might have sent a ransom note to our parents. And then there's Russell. We still don't know how he fits into all this. Oh, come on, Bel! We might even find something that will help us to get out of here."

"Like what?" responded Annabel snappishly. "A ladder?"

Julie looked hard at her. "Let's not quarrel, Bel. That's not going to help."

"I'm sorry, Jool, but I'm so scared. You can't believe how scared I am."

"I know. So am I. But I don't think that man meant to harm us. I think he's got what he was after and he'll leave us alone now."

"But what about the other man? He might not be as considerate as his friend." Julie saw that she was shaking violently. She remembered that Annabel had far more at stake than she had, what with her suspicion of Russell and her anxiety for her mother. She realised that it was up to her to take charge of the situation.

"Look, he's left the electricity on. There's water here. Let's see if we can find a kettle. A good strong cup of coffee would do you good." After only a minute's searching she found what she wanted and they were soon drinking cups of strong, sweet coffee. There was a clock in the room and they saw it was now just after three. Julie's mother wouldn't even have begun to miss them yet.

They went through all the cupboards and all the

drawers, searching for anything that might be of use in getting out. They tried to pick the lock with scissors and a knife, and to knock off the door handle with a heavy brass paperweight, but they had to abandon everything because their fingers became so sore. They turned their attention to the window and tried to calculate how much rope they could make with strips of clothing, but soon realised that not only would such a rope be too short, it wouldn't be strong enough either. Their situation seemed hopeless. At last Julie said, "We'll just have to sit it out, Bel. We might be able to persuade the man to let us go. We could pretend we don't know what it's all about. He might believe us."

But when Dirk arrived they knew at once that he wasn't the sort of man to listen to anything. He was younger than their original captor, and very much nicer looking, but his pale grey eyes held no promise whatsoever of sympathy. And there was something in his expression as he looked at Annabel that frightened her even more than she had been before. He was obviously irritated at being made an errand boy and threw a bag containing bread and fruit on to the coffee table with a gesture of such spite that both girls flinched and drew into the farthest corner. "You'd better make it last," he said. "I'm not coming here three times a day to play the waiter."

"When *will* you be coming back?" Julie asked, trembling.

"Aha! Clever, but not clever enough. I may be back in an hour, or it may be two days – who knows?

So don't get any ideas into your heads about planning a trap. Right?" His eye fell on the coffee cups. "You've made coffee? Did that fool leave the electricity on?"

"Don't switch it off, please!" Annabel begged. The thought of being there all night without a light frightened her more than anything.

"Don't be stupid, little girl," he said softly, coming forward. "Or are you not so stupid, after all? A light in the window might draw attention to your predicament, mightn't it?" Suddenly he bent down and took her chin in his hand, none too gently. He stared intently at her face and said, "Have you by any chance got an older sister?"

"No."

"A pity. Never mind, in a few years' time I might come back and look you up." He laughed unpleasantly and pushed her away, so that she fell backwards on the floor. Then he went away.

"I hate him!" Annabel said. "I hate him a thousand times more than I hate the other one." They heard his footsteps going down the stairs, doors opening and closing as he looked for the main switch, then the front door banged and the sound of his car faded away. Julie tried the light switch. Nothing happened. She took a few deep breaths.

"We'd better have something to eat. Then we'd better try and go to sleep before it gets dark."

But neither of them could eat much. And when midnight came they were both still lying awake wondering if there was any way their parents or the police could work out where they were.

In the morning Julie was awake long before Annabel. They had peered at the clock at three a.m., and it had been some time after four when they had dropped into a deep sleep, worn out with anxiety and fear and hopelessness. Because of her height, Julie had slept on the settee, while Annabel had curled up in one armchair, with her legs on another. Julie didn't disturb her friend. She got up and went over to the book shelf, wishing she could make a cup of tea.

During the night certain ideas had come into her mind, but they had been vague and hardly worth mentioning to Annabel, who in any case was no longer interested in the cause of their capture, merely in the possibility of their getting out. Bird-watching, thought Julie as her eye ranged along the shelf. There were books there which she knew instinctively were not for her eyes, and these she ignored. It was the bird-watching books that interested her.

From what her friend had told her about the late Nick Lestor, and from what she herself had seen of him, it didn't seem likely that he had a love of anything or anybody but himself, let alone birds. She knew that Russell Barnes was keen on that sort of thing, so why couldn't he and Nick have used a common interest in the subject to form some kind of friendship? What *was* Nick's interest in birds all about? Was it possible that Simon had been right about the spying, and that the bird books were some kind of code? She took down *A Field Guide in Colour to Birds*. There again were the mysterious figures and numbers. Surely they wouldn't form a part of ordinary bird-watching, however keen you were?

Annabel started to move. Julie watched her as she stared for a moment at her surroundings and then, realising where she was, sat up with a face that had gone dead white. Her first words were, "Has he come back?"

"Not yet. Are you hungry?"

"No."

"Neither am I, but I think we ought to eat something. If we do manage to think of a way to get out, we'll need all our strength."

"I wonder what our parents are doing?" Annabel said. She tried to swallow a piece of bread, but her mouth was dry and she had to spit it out. She went to the drinks cabinet and brought out a bottle of lemonade. She poured two glasses and when they had managed to eat and drink a little, she said, "Do you think they'll have been told – my mum and Russell?"

"I should think so."

"They'll be out of their minds with worry."

"I know. We've got to get out – we've got to. Nobody knows where we are, and if those men don't come back, we might be here for days." They were silent for a long time, then Annabel said, "Simon should be back now."

"That's it!" Julie cried. "That's our only hope. If Simon tells them what we suspected, surely they'll work it out. They'll see the card from your Uncle Tom and they'll connect it all just like we did!" They hugged each other, hope flooding their hearts for the first time since their capture. "It won't take them long," Julie said eagerly. "They should be here before the man comes back."

Neither of them knew that Brogden had pocketed Uncle Tom's card.

"I was looking at the books when you were asleep," Julie said after they had washed the sleep from their faces and thrown open the window for a breath of fresh air.

"Were you?" Annabel wasn't greatly interested. Julie would read in the middle of an earthquake. It was a wonder she hadn't stopped to read the notice board in the playing field when the man had run after her.

"Listen, Bel. I wasn't just reading, I was trying to work something out." She tried to explain what she had in mind, but somehow when she put it into words it sounded stupid.

Annabel had taken the glasses to the washbasin to rinse them out, and was hardly listening to what her friend was saying. Now she was pinning all her hopes on Simon's powers of deduction. She had faith in Simon. Suddenly she heard Julie exclaim, "Look, Bel! Look!"

"What is it?"

"It's a tranny." Julie fiddled with the buttons and pop music came thumping out. She had tuned in to the local radio station.

"What good will that do us?"

"Cheer us up."

Annabel forced a smile. "I don't want to be cheered up."

"Oh, come on, Bel!"

The music stopped. Local news came on. Something about a one day strike at a paper-mill, and then an item that was halfway through before they understood what it was. "That's us!" gasped Annabel. "We're on the radio!"

"Ssh!"

". . . so, if the missing schoolgirls are, as the police believe, hiding out somewhere locally, please, Annabel and Julie, get in touch with your parents. They're anxious about you and they love you very much, okay? A dog that saved his master's life when fire broke out at his home, was yesterday rewarded with . . ."

Julie switched off. The two girls looked at each other in dismay. "Hiding out?" whispered Annabel. "What do they mean by that?"

"Didn't you hear what they said at the beginning?"

"No. I didn't realise it was us they were talking about. It never occurred to me that we might be on the radio."

"They said the police believed we'd run away because you'd never really got over the loss of your dad, and couldn't face up to having a stepfather – something like that. It was put in a nice way, but that's what they were getting at. Oh, Bel, don't you see what's happened? They think we've run away of our own accord. They'll never come here looking for us now. Even if Simon's told them what he thinks, they obviously don't believe him."

"There's Uncle Tom's card. Mum might decide to come and get Uncle Nick's stuff."

"In the middle of all this? Would you? They'll be hanging over the phone, not bothering about a selfish old man. So there's only one thing to do now. We've got to find some way of getting out. We've got to be away from here before that man comes back. Now it's been on the radio it's sure to have been in the papers as well, and he'll be dead scared. He might think of getting rid of us. So we've got to find something, anything, to make a rope. Here's a couple of tea towels for a start. Move, Bel, for heaven's sake! We don't know how soon it might be before he gets here!"

Chapter Ten

Nothing was further from Annabel's mother's thoughts than the card from Uncle Tom. Annabel had mentioned it briefly on the telephone, along with the others, but she had said nothing about the message regarding Uncle Nick's things. All the acknowledgements, the thank you letters, the little boxes of wedding cake, would be sent out later, when this terrible business was sorted out. She didn't even notice that the card wasn't there among all the others standing on the windowsills.

"Tell me again, Simon," Russell said, "exactly what happened when you went to the flat in River Street."

"Well, nothing much," Simon said. "Annabel wanted us to go with her because she'd been scared the last time she'd gone there."

"Why was she scared?" asked Russell.

"She said she had a feeling that somebody was watching her. At first we laughed about it. We thought she was – well, sorry, Mrs Pedrick – Mrs Barnes, I mean – seeing ghosts. It wasn't until days later that she remembered somebody standing by the garages. He was wearing a trenchcoat like the man who chased after Julie. I know the policeman didn't believe me. At least, if he believed me, he thought it was just a coincidence. I suppose lots of men of your age, Russell, wear coats like that. I mean, I'm sorry, I didn't . . ." He was getting very confused.

"It's okay, Simon. I'm not offended. I'm forty years old and there's not much I can do about it. But I've never actually worn a trenchcoat, as it happens." He smiled, putting the young man at his ease. "I know what you mean. He was a man about my age, you think?"

"Well, gosh, I didn't know you were forty. I thought the man was about thirty."

"Right, we're getting somewhere. A man about thirty, watching the flat. And by the way, I shouldn't underestimate the police if I were you. They'll check it all out."

Mrs Barnes was twisting her hands together. She looked pale and drawn. "What does it all mean, Russell?" she asked. "You're so calm about it all. What do you know that you haven't told me?"

"I haven't told you what I did before I met you."

"What do you mean? You're not mixed up in all this, are you?"

"In a way I am. I'm sorry, love. I didn't want to cause any family disruptions, but I had certain suspicions about your brother. But let's take it step by step and you'll begin to understand my position. What happened next, Simon?"

"Well, the next thing was that that creep chased Julie across the fields and pinched her bag."

"No, before that. Let's deal first with the visit to the flat. Tell me exactly what you did."

"Oh, yes – the maps. The Ordance Survey maps. They're all marked with signs of one sort or another, but we couldn't make any sense of them. I've got them at home. Would you like to see them?"

"Later. I can guess what they were used for. What else did you say you brought away with you?"

"Just some bits of Sellotape and pens, paper clips. Oh – and Julie brought the books. They were books on ornithology. One of them was a small one, about that size –" he demonstrated with his hands – "and Julie popped it in her bag. When she was chased and the man took her bag, we thought it was the book he was after, but it didn't seem all that likely. It was just a thought, you know?" He was feeling uncomfortable now, for he would soon have to admit that Annabel had been snooping around in her mother's bedroom.

"And what made you alter your mind about the importance of the book?"

Simon took a deep breath and spoke in a rush. "Annabel looked at Nick's things."

"What things?"

"In the box – upstairs."

"There's no upstairs in the flat," said Mrs Barnes.

"No, upstairs here."

"Oh, you mean in my wardrobe? Annabel looked in the box in my wardrobe?" She looked agitated and bit her lip.

"Annabel brought the box downstairs one night. That night when you went out to dinner. There was a book in it about the same size as the one Julie put in her bag."

"And you thought the man might have mistaken Julie's book for Nick's? That was very smart," said Russell.

"Was it?" Simon was pleased at the compliment and went on with more confidence. "We thought the figures in the book tied in with the markings on the map."

"They probably did."

"You really think so? Great!"

"I'll go and get the box," Mrs Barnes said, eager to do anything that might help. When she returned she put it down on the floor and took the contents out, one by one. After a few moments her face took on a puzzled look. "It's not here," she said.

Russell didn't say, "Are you sure?" His eyes passed quickly over the items on the floor and he said to Simon, "Do you think the girls might have taken it?"

"They might have, if they were bored and had thought of something they wanted to check on."

"Is there anything else you can remember about your visit to the flat? Anything that the man might have wanted, besides the book?"

"You know there wasn't, Russell," Mrs Barnes said. "You went with me the day after the funeral. If there had been anything you would have seen it then."

"Not necessarily. At that particular time I didn't want to appear to be too involved. I was thinking of your feelings." He turned to Simon, who had suddenly opened his mouth to speak. "What is it?"

"There was a telephone call."

"When you were in the flat?"

"Yes. Annabel wouldn't answer it, but I did."

"Who was it?"

"He didn't say. But I didn't like his tone of voice, so I hung up on him."

"Tell me exactly what he said."

"All I can remember is that he said, 'Is Nick there?' and I said no, he wasn't, and he asked when he would be back. I said he wouldn't be back, and he said what the hell did I mean by that? So I hung up."

"You can't remember anything special about his voice, I suppose?"

"No, I can't. I'm sorry."

"Don't worry. We'll make sense of all this before we've finished. Now I'll tell you my side of the story." He took his wife's hand. "I'm sorry about this, love, and if I'd known that there was any possibility of the girls being involved, of course I would have told you. The truth is, I'm afraid Nick was doing something illegal."

"What kind of thing?" Mrs Barnes asked.

"I think he was involved in egg piracy."

"So that's it!" said Simon.

"Egg piracy?" said Mrs Barnes in a flat voice.

"Yes. To the layman it sounds silly, unimportant, but given the right market and the right product, there's sometimes a lot of money in it. But it isn't the money that matters."

"What are you talking about?" said Mrs Barnes. "Was Nick stealing consignments of eggs, or something, and selling them on the black market?"

"No, love. I'm not talking about that kind of egg, I'm talking about the eggs of rare and endangered birds."

"Oh!" said Simon, "I've got it! When I was in Cornwall, somebody was talking about reintroducing the chough to the cliffs down there, because it's the county emblem. They said there was a rumour that it had been tried and somebody had stolen the eggs. There used to be thousands of pairs nesting on the cliffs, but now there isn't a single pair."

"I was involved in trying to track down the men who stole those eggs," Russell said, "but we lost them. It was one of the greatest disappointments of my life. I'd have forfeited a year's salary to get them."

"*You* were involved?" repeated Mrs Barnes. "How?"

"At that time I was Chief Investigative Officer with an international bird protection society – the first one to be set up as a secret unit to try and combat the illegal traffic in birds' eggs and birds of prey. And I loved my job, I make no bones about that. I did it because I thought it was important. I felt such people were despicable, and I still do. I'm very sorry that Nick should have had a part in it, but I'm beginning to be more and more convinced that he was the co-ordinator of a worldwide traffic in eggs."

"It all makes sense now, doesn't it?" said Simon. "The account book and the maps, and the girls' disappearance."

In a low voice Mrs Barnes said, "Are you telling me that the girls have been kidnapped by a gang of international crooks? You've known that all along and you haven't informed the police?"

"I have informed them," Russell said, "but they've agreed to keep that aspect of the case to themselves until they have more facts to go on. But you can be sure they're checking it out. I've worked with them before and their computer records have been of immense value. As for my involvement, my enquiries led me to Nick, but I couldn't prove anything. Then when I met you and I realised you were Nick's sister I was torn between two loyalties. I'd always intended to give it up when I was forty and hand over the job to my deputy, who's thirteen years my junior and has the stamina to spend days on end tracking down pirates over some of the roughest terrain in the world. When Nick was killed I had already handed in my resignation. The unit found me another job within the society."

"Nick was killed rock-climbing," Simon said. "Was he after birds' eggs at the time?"

"We think so," Russell replied. "There were red kites in the area."

"Red kites! RK! That was one of the sets of initials in the book – and on the maps! We thought they were people's initials. We thought . . ."

"What did you think, Simon?" asked Mrs Barnes.

"We thought Nick was either running an illegal betting shop or that he was blackmailing people. I'm sorry, Mrs Barnes, but you did ask."

"Don't apologise. When I tried to make sense of the book I thought the same thing. But then I thought, let the dead rest in peace. I didn't think any good could come of raking it all up. So I left the book where it was and tried to forget all about it. If only I hadn't! If only I'd told you, you would have known what to do about it."

Simon said, "Is there so much money to be had for birds' eggs that people are prepared to risk their lives to get them? It doesn't seem possible."

"It isn't always the money, Simon. With some people it seems to be a compulsion, like climbing mountains because they're there. As long as they know there are eggs to be had, they've got to get them. On the other hand, if you're out of work or earning a poor salary for a boring job, the money can be very important, little as it may be. But in this particular case, I believe – although I can't prove it yet – that some person or persons unknown are so fanatically keen to extend their collection, that they will pay almost any price to get what they want. And it may well be that this unknown person is so anxious to keep his dealings from the public gaze that he has employed an agent to act as go-between. Some years ago there was a professor working on a project at one of the top American universities who was being supplied with the egg whites of large numbers of highly-protected birds. He needed only the whites of the eggs because he was working on research into albumen. This man knew that what he was doing was wrong, but he was so interested in his subject and so keen to produce his thesis on it, that he considered himself above the law. He enlisted the services of just such a man as Nick Lestor, who was incapable of appreciating the damage he was doing to the wild bird populations of the world. The peregrine falcon, the fastest and most beautiful bird of prey in the world, has declined dramatically in numbers with the use of insecticides, yet this was one of the birds the professor was interested in. His agent supplied him with the eggs – to my mind one of the most contemptible crimes that can be committed against any wild creature."

There was silence in the room for a few minutes. Mrs Barnes broke it at last. "If Nick was doing that," she said, "he should be exposed, dead or not. Go and get the maps, Simon, and let's see if we can make anything out of the letters and figures you talked of. Who knows? They might give us a clue as to where the girls are."

Chapter Eleven

"I can't do any more," Annabel said, holding out her blistered hands. "Haven't we got enough yet?"

"No," Julie sighed. "It's got to stretch to about two metres from the ground. We don't want to break our legs when we jump the last bit, and then we've got to have enough to come right over the windowsill and across the room to the washbasin, so we can tie it to the pipe. There's nothing else we could tie it to."

They had started with the towels. They had been too bulky to tie into knots, so they had cut them into strips. When they had tested the strength of it, the rope had torn apart. The curtains were no use, either; they were of very heavy velvet and the scissors were too blunt to cut them. The next thing they tried was the material from the chair cushions. Each strip was no more than half a metre long, and once the knots had been tied, there was very little additional length in the rope. With the scissors so blunt and the material so tough, both girls were now suffering sore and blistered fingers. They had to admit that if they did any more cutting their hands would be too sore to use the rope.

It was a shock to realise that it was now well into the afternoon and they were not much nearer freedom than they had been last night. For a short while they consoled themselves with a piece of bread and the box of chocolate mints. They listened to the radio, but the news bulletin made no mention of them. They began to feel that they had been forgotten, or that their parents had accepted the police theory that they had simply run away from home and would contact them before long.

Julie said, "I think I might be able to drop about ten feet without hurting myself."

"*I* couldn't."

Julie didn't look at her friend as she added, "What I meant was that I could jump and go for help."

Annabel sprang to her feet in panic. "Julie, you wouldn't leave me here on my own! You wouldn't!"

"I don't see any other way."

"But what if you met him in the lane? You couldn't outrun him because he's got a car, and I'd be left on my own with him. Oh, Julie, don't!"

"What's in the other direction, down the track?"

"Just woods, and then a quarry. Beyond that is the big house."

"Witherley, where Lord Scawby lives? How far is it?"

"I won't tell you."

"All right, forget it. It was just a thought."

They lapsed into silence, fearing to quarrel. The afternoon wore on. The sky was overcast, but there was no rain. "It'll be dark early tonight," Annabel said. "What time was it when he came yesterday?"

"About five, I think."

"We haven't got much time. Let's try the chair behind the door again and hit him when he comes in."

"We've been through all that before. We're not strong enough to knock him out, and that's the only way we'd get away from him."

Annabel got up and walked about the room. Julie noticed that she was rubbing the side of her thigh. "What's the matter with your leg?" she asked.

"Oh, when he pushed me down on the floor I got a bruise. There was ridge, or a loose floorboard or something under the carpet and I fell right on it . . ." She broke off as the same thought occurred to both of them at once.

"We might be able to get through to the room below!" cried Julie.

They had to push the settee to the other side of the room in order to roll back the carpet. Even their sore fingers didn't deter them now, so eager were they to try their new idea. There were certainly loose boards, with every sign of their having been recently moved. The two girls got down on their hands and knees and were soon staring into the dark cavity below. Julie felt around with her hands. "There's something in here," she exclaimed. "Boxes." She took out a long, slim box, made of wood and hinged on one side, with rusting clasps at the other. She laid it on the floor and opened it.

"Birds' eggs," said Annabel in disappointment, who had hoped it would contain something that might help them to get out. "Just a kid's collection – typical of Uncle Nick to hide it away like that."

Julie's thought were running in quite a different direction. "I read somewhere," she said, "that some people steal rare birds' eggs and sell them to collectors. That's what this is all about! That's what your Uncle Nick was doing!"

"Does it matter? It doesn't help us."

"No, but at least we know what his nasty little secret was." She pulled out a second box, identical to the first then a third and a fourth. Each contained carefully arranged and docketed eggs, every one resting in its own little cup to guard against damage. In all there were about two hundred eggs.

The sheer number and variety of the eggs gave a different complexion to Julie's last words. The girls were of a generation that cared about conservation and the protection of wildlife, and Annabel felt deeply ashamed that a relation of hers had been involved in egg piracy.

Now she knew that she had to get out even if it meant throwing herself out of the window. It didn't matter now if she killed herself. She couldn't face up to everybody at school knowing what her uncle had been. Their school had even won a national award for a conservation project last year, and she had worked as hard as anybody to secure it.

And then, all in a moment, the entire situation changed as Julie pulled out a length of rope from the cavity beneath them! Nick had stored his spare climbing gear under the floorboards, safe from casual observation. That, perhaps, was the rubbbish to which Uncle Tom had referred.

The rope was slender but strong, being made of nylon. It was quite new. Annabel ran to the window and flung it open. Julie said, "Just a minute – we've got to tie some knots in it at intervals, so we can grip them as we go down. If we don't, we'll tear the skin off our hands."

Never had five minutes dragged so slowly as Julie feverishly tied the knots. All the time, the girls were listening for the sound of a car crunching over the gravel forecourt. Then Julie said, "Do you want to go first?"

"No, you go. I'll watch how you do it." Now that the moment for release was so near, Annabel's rash thoughts of jumping out of the window had evaporated, and all she felt was an old, terrible fear of heights.

Julie went backwards out of the window, confident in her strength. Hand over hand, she dropped away from her friend. Just as she reached the ground, the sound they had been dreading all day came to their ears. Their enemy had come back. Annabel's mouth went completely dry. She tried to swallow, but couldn't. "Come on!" cried Julie urgently. "Come on, Bel – it's easy."

At last, and even as she heard the man's footsteps on the stairs, Annabel forced herself out of the window. Shaking in every limb, she was sure that at every knot she would make a mistake. She heard the door of the room open, heard the man's exclamation as he realised what had happened, and before she had reached the ground, saw his face above her, white with fury.

Dirk, too, had a fear of heights. He shouted a curse and turned from the window. As he ran downstairs the girls were making their way across the overgrown garden at the back of the house. They climbed over a fence and found themselves in dense woodland. Julie could have gone much quicker if she had been on her own but she couldn't leave her friend behind. Together they tripped over fallen logs, fell into brambles, twisted their feet on the uneven ground, but kept on. Behind them they could hear the crashing of the man's feet as he blundered along. Terrified and breathless, the girls knew there was no place to hide. Darkness was coming on fast. "Where now?" gasped Julie as they came to a path which forked left and right. Annabel pointed. All she could think of was that the path she had indicated led to the quarry, and beyond the quarry was the home of Lord Scawby. He would help them. He would know what to do.

They blundered out into the quarry with startling suddenness, and the great, wide expanse spread out before them brought them to a dismayed halt. Where to go now? They ought to have kept to the track to the left instead of the old road which had once carried the traffic to the quarry. Annabel groaned. She felt so small, so helpless. "We've got to climb, Bel, it's all we can do," Julie said. She grabbed her friend's arm and pulled her towards the opposite end of the quarry, where the face rose up jagged and scarred before them.

An owl flew overhead, not making a sound, and there were bats too – creatures which had seldom been disturbed over the past few years. The clouds were drifting away now, revealing stars beginning to brighten as the darkness fell. At any other time it would have been a tranquil scene, a picture for an artist.

It was not even a well-matched contest, for although Julie could have held her own with the young man, Annabel was out of her class. She had reached the extent of her physical resources. She couldn't go on.

"You can make it!" Julie panted. "You can, you can! Just to the rock face and then we'll climb."

Annabel hadn't even the breath to protest that the man would climb after them. But Julie, having glanced backwards as they ran across the garden, had seen what Annabel hadn't – that their captor had been afraid to shin down the rope that was hanging so conveniently from the window. He was, she suspected, afraid of heights. It was all she could pin her hopes on.

Miraculously they reached the rocks and began to climb, Julie first in order to find the best handholds and to give her friend a tug upwards now and then. They heard their pursuer beneath them: Annabel gave a strangled little scream as he grabbed her foot. She was clinging to a substantial hold with both hands, and as he tugged at her right foot she kicked out desperately, wildly, with her left. It was enough to unbalance him.

The man fell, taking Annabel's right shoe with him. There was a soft thud, and he was on the ground, swearing and gasping with pain. Looking down, Julie saw that he was holding his shoulder. Even at that distance she could see that it was either badly wrenched or dislocated. She gave Annabel a swift, encouraging grin, and pulled her up to the next course. They had beaten him off! For the time being, at least, they were safe.

But they had to climb higher, much higher, out of reach and if possible out of sight. Julie didn't dare to suggest to her friend that the man might have a gun. At last they came to rest on a wide rocky ledge two-thirds of the height of the quarry. Annabel was in a state of terror – she daren't look down. Julie told her to lie down with her back against the rock, and after a few minutes she began to feel better. "Where is he?" she asked.

"He's limped off to the other side of the quarry," Julie said. "I think he's quite badly hurt, Bel. He won't be able to get up here."

"But if he can get back to his car, he might fetch the other man."

"From what I saw of his shoulder he won't be able to drive."

"You don't know, Julie. You don't know. And what are we going to do? Nobody knows we're here. And there's no way I'm going to climb back down there."

Julie was looking upwards. "I'm going up," she said, "on my own."

"No!" cried Annabel. "If you go I'm going with you."

"You know you can't. You've only got one shoe, and your hands are much worse than mine. Don't worry – he won't try to get up here, and even if he does, there are plenty of loose rocks on the ledge. You can fling them down at him. It can't be very far to the big house. I can be there in ten minutes and call the police."

Annabel knew she was right. Julie was tougher than she was. They had had two days of terror, they had had very little food, and they hadn't slept much. A night on the quarry face would be more than either of them could bear, even though the ledge was almost two metres wide and quite safe. She nodded, and Julie began to climb.

After a few minutes she heard Julie's triumphant voice. "I'm at the top, Bel. I'm okay. I'll be back with help before long."

And then silence.

Chapter Twelve

Julie knew she had torn a ligament. There was no point in denying it and trying to ignore it. The pain was so keen that she couldn't put her left foot to the ground, and she was still trembling.

She groaned. So near and yet so far – she could see the lights of the house less than half a mile away. She had tried crawling on hands and knees, but her hands were so blistered from using the blunt scissors, and from cuts sustained on the quarry face, that it was agony to use them. It was too far away for anyone at the house to hear her cries, yet still too near the quarry for her to dare use her voice. If Annabel heard her she would feel hopeless and lost, might even panic and try to reach her. And that could lead to disaster. So she kept silent.

She was sitting now with her back against a stone wall, taking deep breaths and trying to summon all her strength to make one last desperate attempt to hop. Another thought occurred to her. She took off her socks and put them on her hands, slipped her feet back into her trainers, and rolled over once more on to her knees. She tested the roughly-bandaged hands. Better, but still excruciatingly painful. How far could she get?

And then her stomach seemed to turn right over. Coming from the other side of the wall were noises – the unmistakeable sounds of someone blundering over the ground. She dropped flat, hoping that the gathering darkness would conceal her from any casual glance over the wall. Had Annabel been right? Had the man managed to get back to his car and go for assistance? Had he seen her progress up the last part of the quarry face? And was his accomplice now looking for her, here in the gloom, in open country, as she had been just a few short weeks before? She held her breath and waited.

There was a snort.

She looked, raised herself on her knees, and laughed aloud.

"Hello horse!" she said.

Julie was an athletic girl, with Olympic ambitions. but she had lived all her life in a suburban close in a manufacturing town. She didn't know the first thing about horses, except that they had a head at one end and a tail at the other and four vicious-looking feet shod with iron.

But the horse didn't know that. As far as he was concerned she was welcome company and a possible source of goodies. He tossed his head and flicked his tail and waited. For a few moments they looked at each other in speculation, then Julie drew in a long, deep breath, blew it out again, and said, "Oh, hell! Why not?"

She pulled herself up the wall and slung one leg over. The horse did a sort of three-point turn and looked at her again. "Come here," she said. "Come *here*!"

To her amazement, he came. He appeared quite docile. She held out her hand. As he came forward for the expected treat she somehow managed to grab his mane, push herself off the wall with one foot and get the other one over his back. That was the moment when real terror struck her. She was actually riding a horse! What in heaven's name did she do next? As he walked around the field she clung on as they say a drowning man clutches a straw. It was only by sheer good luck that she had got on facing his head.

And luck favoured her again. A sudden pain shot through her injured leg and as she jerked it upwards her foot seemed to convey the required instruction to him. He went on at a much smarter pace, towards a gate at the far end of the field – and to her delight, much closer to the lights of the house. When they reached the gate there was just enough light for her to see the rope that secured it to the gatepost. She leaned forward, tossed it aside, and pulled at the gate. It opened a fraction. After a great deal of trial and error, she discovered that tugging one side of his mane seemed to have the effect of turning him in the same direction. It took perhaps ten minutes for her to guide him past the gate close enough for her to lean over and give it a good hard pull. The rest he did himself. He knew what was on the other side.

In the house was his best friend in all the world. And near the house was a patch of grass the like of which he seldom encountered. Left unmown until the wild flowers had seeded, it was a horse's paradise. But even more tempting was the flowerbed ranged beneath the magnificent staircase. Once he had reached it, thought Julie, not even Princess Anne could have moved him.

She fell off. She was sick. She sat on her bottom and pulled herself painfully up the stairs and along the stone terrace to the light that streamed from the French windows. She managed to get to her feet and turn the handle. The door yielded. "I'm sorry," she said to the man inside. "Your horse is eating your tulips."

Then she fainted.

Simon and Russell were on their way to Scawby. Once the idea had come to them they had lost no time. "Try to imagine what the girls might have found out," Russell had said, and Simon had replied that they could only have deciphered the meaning of the mysterious symbols in the maps and in the book.

121

They had gone over it again and again. The letters on the maps made perfect sense to Russell, each letter or combination of letters being the initial letters of a bird's name, and the numbers being the number of eggs taken from each particular site. So far, so good. Without the book they were seriously hampered, but as both Simon and Mrs Barnes could remember some of the figures in it, it appeared to Russell to have been merely Nick's account book of moneys received.

"There must have been something else," Russell urged. "Something that made them go and investigate. Could they possibly have remembered something about Nick?"

And then Mrs Barnes, almost casually, had said, "I suppose it's possible that Nick kept some of his things at Uncle Tom's house."

"Uncle Tom's house?" repeated Russell.

"You remember – it was Uncle Tom who brought him up." But that had been about the extent of Russell's knowledge of Uncle Tom. The fact that he had a house at Scawby had gone over his head, if it had been mentioned at all. Russell was a stranger to the Midland counties of England, so even if Scawby had been talked of, he wouldn't have realised it was so near. Neither Annabel nor her mother had talked much about the old man since the row at the nursing home.

When Mrs Barnes discovered that the key to the Scawby house was missing from the box where she had put it, they knew they were on to something, and when she said there was no telephone in the house, all three of them agreed that the girls must have gone there for reasons of their own, and got locked in. It didn't seem likely that they had been forced to get the key and go with the thieves; somebody in the close would have seen something. Anyhow, Mrs Briers had watched them go, had seen them catch the bus.

As they turned into the drive Simon shouted, "There's a car in front of the house!"

Russell made no comment. He drew up his own car and got out. "Stay here," he said. "I'll go and investigate."

Simon got out and gave Russell a hard look. "No way," he said. "I'm going with you."

"They may have had an – accident. And we don't know whose car that is."

"I'm going in with you. I've got to. Don't you see that?"

"Which one of the girls is so important to you, Simon?"

The boy was sufficiently mature not to blush. "Both of them," he said, and added, "but Annabel's – special."

"Come on then."

They went into the house. They didn't call out. They could feel there was nobody there. They looked in all the downstairs rooms, went upstairs, and then to the attic. The open window and the rope attached to the water pipe told their own story. Simon said,

"That's Julie's anorak. They were here."

Russell looked out of the window and pointed out the obvious route which the girls had taken through the weedy growth of two years' neglect. They had obviously fled from the driver of the car. "Come on," he said. "We'd better follow them."

It was growing dark as they set off. The girls were at that moment crouching on the quarry ledge, and as they followed the trail, Julie was beginning her climb to the top of the quarry.

When the man and the boy reached the quarry they almost fell over the inert body of Dirk Van Hoof. Russell bent over him. "I know this character," he said.

"Is he – dead?"

"Oh, no – he'll live to give me some very important information." He bent closer as Dirk began to stir. "The two girls!" he demanded. "Where are they?"

Dirk said something in one of his many languages. Simon didn't understand, but Russell did. His face hardened. He grasped the injured man by his sagging shoulder. "Tell me where they are!"

Dirk raised his uninjured arm. "Up there," he said. "Get me a doctor."

The light was fading fast, but the clouds were beginning to clear. They strained their eyes to scan the face of the quarry. Suddenly Simon pointed. "There!" he said. "I can see something yellow. Annabel has a yellow sweater."

Russell said, "Take off this man's shoes and fling them as far away from him as you can, then find something to tie his ankles together. I don't want to lose him. Here – here's my tie, use this." Simon knew that this time there was no arguing with the older man. He bent down to carry out his instructions. Dirk was by now semi-conscious again.

At the quarry face, Russell called, "Annabel! Julie! Are you there?" For a few moments there was silence. He called again. After another pause there was a movement as somebody fluttered a light garment from high up on the wall of the quarry, and a thin voice floated down to him, though the words were indistinct. "I'm coming up!" he called.

Forty years old or not, Russell was a healthy and active man. He had done a great deal of climbing during his years with the bird protection unit, and the quarry was little more than a steep climb to him. In spite of the increasing darkness he had no trouble in finding holds for his hands and feet. He pulled himself on to the ledge, and his face muscles tensed. "Where's Julie?" he said.

"She's gone up," Annabel whispered. "Gone to get help." Then her face contorted, tears sprang to her eyes, and she held out her arms. "Oh, Russell!" she said.

"It's all right, sweetheart, it's all right," her stepfather said gently, holding her tight. "You'll soon be out of here."

"Where's Julie?" said another voice.

They turned their heads. "I thought I told you not to come up here," Russell said.

"No, you didn't," Simon retorted. "You told me

to tie up the man down there. I've done that. By the way, I think I've learned a new swear word in a foreign language. Hullo, Bel!"

She held out one hand. Simon took it. "I won't ask again where Julie is," he said. "If she'd fallen down you two wouldn't be looking so cheerful." He looked up. "Is that the way she went?"

Annabel nodded.

"I'd better go and see if she's all right," said Russell. He looked at Simon. "Take care of Annabel."

"I always have," said Simon. "I always will."

An hour later it was all over. Russell had met the rescue team who had been alerted by Lord Scawby. Julie had received treatment for her torn ligament. Annabel and Simon had been lifted by rope, much to the indignant protests of the latter, who had wanted to prove to his girlfriend that he was as competent at rock-climbing as Russell Barnes. Parents and police agreed that in view of the pending investigations into the egg robberies, it would be as well to circulate the story that the girls had simply got themselves locked into a relative's isolated house. And in time the whole episode was forgotten, except by those who had been most closely involved.

When Jan Van Hoof came to trial nearly two years

later, the world's press was completely unaware that three young people from a small town in the English Midlands had been responsible for alerting the bird-loving world to a vital part of the network that supplied him with his plunder. Van Hoof was a leading figure in the diplomatic world, long-serving President of one of the world's most prestigious bird protection societies, and a rich and powerful man.

His weakness had its roots in pride. He had wanted to own the most comprehensive private collection of birds' eggs in the world. As a boy in his native Netherlands he had started innocently enough, watching the shore birds nesting near his home on the coast near Rotterdam. A few eggs – ringed plover, oystercatcher, turnstone – had started the craze; then another boy at his school, hearing of his interest, had offered for sale a collection made by his father, but in which he had had little interest himself. The price had been high, but young Jan came from a wealthy family. He always had plenty of pocket money and indulged his fancies. Word got around that Van Hoof would pay well for new items for his collection, and over the next few years he added to it almost every week.

When the leading natural historians began to feel more and more concerned about declining bird populations, and governments began to pass laws forbidding the taking of eggs, Van Hoof's activities went underground. He joined, and worked actively in, many wildlife projects, making connections, sniffing out those people whose love of money outweighed their concern for the environment. And eventually he met a young Englishman by the name of Nick Lestor, who was willing to risk a great deal for a pitiful reward.

For Nick Lestor, as his family were the first to admit, had no outstanding intellectual abilities. He was a man of his own class with no ambitions to climb higher. The ability to pay for a round of drinks in his local pub, to eat well, and to spend the occasional high-living weekend, was the height of his aspirations. The rest of the time he preferred to walk alone. His name was only briefly mentioned at Van Hoof's trial. As a dead man he could scarcely answer the accusations made against him.

As it happened, he was not, as Russell had surmised, the co-ordinator of the network. Most of his unscrupulous associates knew him merely as a man who could find markets for their loot. The real king-pin turned out to be a man called Brogden, who had got away with several million guilders, changed his name, and disappeared. It was said that he had no interest whatsoever in birds' eggs, and it was unlikely that his next venture would have anything to do with them. To amass a huge fortune and act out the part of a powerful yet mysterious figure was his only motive. The police in several countries are still looking for him.

As for Nick Lestor, it was never discovered where, or with whom, he had spent his ill-gotten gains. That was the secret the dead man took with him to his grave.